so man- lights!

was this a garden?

reception west
w/ the Baron's papers

football emporium

courtyard

purl gate

dirty hallway

map room

X

to Tarmac

spher

elevator to basement

dogleg hallway

reception south

Beautiful

ZURT

Send Coffee Books
http://www.sendcoffee.com/publishing.html

Cover design © Minorsage
Cover images: silhouette - katagaci & barunpatro
www.rgbstock.com

Publisher's Cataloging-in-Publication data
Simon, Jes.
Beautiful Zurt / Jes Simon.
p. cm.
ISBN 978-0-9837042-3-2
1. Science Fiction. 2. Adventure fiction. 3. Diary fiction.
4. Technology and civilization--Fiction. I. Title.

813.6--dc22

First Edition: February 2014

10 9 8 7 6 5 4 3 2 1

"If a Baezene asks to borrow credits, always lend them.

They will quickly pay them back.

It's a test of trust."

Baron Tarris Hylke

Beautiful

ZURT

Jes Simon

a novella

Send Coffee® Books

SEVEN DAYS IN

Curse you, Baron Hylke! This is dreadful. I guess, if you've found this journal, you know that already. I've always written my journals to my future self. This time, I'm not sure who will read this. Nonce, I hope it's my future self.

This is not the lush resort the Baron told me I would find. In all the years I've known him, I've never had him lie to me so horribly. His message said it was luxurious – hiking, games, adventure. *"Come join me, Renya. You'll love it!"* he scrawled on the postcard, attaching a file with the coordinates. I was ready for a vacation – instead, I am marooned. His ship orbits above, like mine, but is equally as useless. No signal on the mobile com from the Baron's ship or mine. I don't understand what shut my ship down. None of the controls would respond. No way to stop it. All I could do was teleport down to the planets surface. I grabbed my escape bag and anything in arms length. I thought once I got here he'd explain what was going on, but he's nowhere to be found.

It's been seven days – a week. I haven't found the Baron. I haven't found anyone. I've been through all the ground level buildings a thousand times. I found the Baron's papers, here in one of the main buildings, scattered about on the long desk in one of the reception rooms. There are notes and photos, but nothing says 'Renya, here's how you teleport off!'. Nothing.

There are alien tools lying all over the place. They have to be important, but how, I don't know. There's a metal rod, pale teal in colour, on the floor of the elevator – every day. The Baron called it a mongoo. I pick it up, attach it to something; the next morning, there it is again. I've started kicking it every time I use the elevator. Stupid mongoo.

The Baron was right about one thing. This Beautiful Zurt is an alluring planet. Shining crystal towers, metallic buildings and walls in all the colours of the rainbow. In some rooms plants have made their way through small gaps, crawling along the ceiling and walls. I don't know where the Baron came up with the name Zurt. Knowing him, it's probably a noise his zipper made once.

There are no signs of life here. The equipment I've found is still working – though I have no way to know its purpose.

I stand corrected. There's a gwirg going by right now. I'm not sure if it qualifies as a sign of life though. It's a silver sphere with an antenna. It comes by every now-and-then – flies into whatever area I'm in with a breathless whirring sound – says something – then flies off. Gwirg is the name the Baron gave it. I've tried to follow it. It goes out of the nearest gate straight into the jungle. Four days ago I took off after it and ended up lost in the jungle for almost a full day. I tried to keep up, but it's fast and the jungle is difficult to navigate.

I thought I might be able to send out a distress signal from the jungle. I couldn't raise a reply from my ship or the Baron's, but I found an open channel to an orbiting transponder. It replied to my query with 'Ready, Baron Hylke'. I recorded a video, uploaded it, and set it to loop. It wouldn't take exact locations to send the message without his passcode, so it's up there broadcasting in the general area. At least, I hope it is.

The distress video took almost all the power left in my mobile com. I always travel with extra batteries and a solar charger – you never know what kind of power an alien planet has available, and I got tired of carrying a pocket full of adapters. The solar charger usually works, but it wasn't in the bags I grabbed when I teleported down. I'm using what power I have left sparingly.

I was lucky to find my way back to the city. I wandered for hours before I came upon a small hillock. The jungle foliage is dense. At ground level I can barely see a double-pace in front of me. There are plants with fronds as large as I am. From the top of the hillock I could see the sparkling towers of the city off in a distance and made my way back. I may try to follow the gwirg again. Whatever it's saying might be important.

MAPPING THE CITY

I've mapped the main buildings of the city. There's no way of knowing how accurate the map is without an aerial view. The buildings and chambers are a bit strange. They appear tall from a distance but not once you've entered them. The gaming halls seem to have the highest ceilings.

When I first hit the ground I went through all the buildings quickly, calling out for the Baron, then for anyone. No one answered. Seeing the notebooks and papers, I thought the Baron must be around somewhere. I have not found that 'somewhere' yet.

I've only mapped the ground floor right now. There's a basement as well. All of the city is surrounded by jungle. The Baron could be somewhere in the jungle, but I haven't ventured far – it's too easy to get lost.

It does look like this was a resort at one time. There's an abandoned garden, reception rooms and game halls – Foon-ball Emporium and Hall of Umflungoo. The Baron left instant photos with the names scrawled on them. It's easier to use his names.

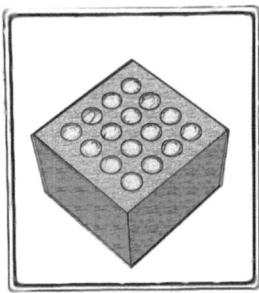

His naming convention ranges from familiar words to ridiculous letter combinations. I don't understand why he decided to name things this way. Why not call the bright red cube 'Bright Red Cube' rather than 'snuge'? His invitation was the first I'd heard from him for over a year. Had he been trapped here so long his mind was off?

I gathered or made most of the tools I could to match the photos he left, setting them side-by-side to get an idea of his names. The Baron left extensive notes on the tools. He must have believed their use was the way off this planet. The tools attach to each other – torkus to gwingus making a wufflar. The wufflar has a button. When you press it another torkus pops out.

There are five tools that seem primary. They're the ones I find laying around all over the place. You can attach them to each other, but you can't break them down into anything else. I've dubbed them 'first level' tools. I've built up to one fourth level item. The Baron called it a cacapoo. Sounds like a type of dog but looks a lot like a green rubber band. I've been using it to put up my hair.

I don't understand how the tools attach and break apart. You take something that looks like a stick of crystal and tap it onto something that looks like a coin and 'BAM!' you have a large ball – a very light large ball. By 'bam' I mean they light up – the area around them lights up for a split second – then there's something completely different where the other two had been. I've never seen this with any of the tools or artifacts I've come across on other planets.

You can break the tools apart again with a series of taps. It took me a while to learn it. It has to be something in their chemical composition. The Baron mentions 'kwish-age engineering'. His notes are vague and infuriating. If he left them for me, he could have been clearer. If this is some game he's playing, watching me knock my head about trying to figure it out, I'll end him.

I decided to map the ground level, because I kept walking in circles. One metallic blue building has a map on the wall, but it's almost completely faded away; mostly just an X with some alien writing that seems to say 'You are Here'. I was going to go through the Baron's papers for a map, but there are so many papers, from small slips with scribbles to large sheets with drawings. He must have been here quite a while. Like I said, he could still be here, somewhere.

The sight of the city from the tarmac, where I landed, is impressive. I didn't realize it when I got here. I was stunned by the silence and ran through the buildings trying to find anyone. Going back through to make the map, I took it all in. From the tarmac you can make out the jungle to the north, east, and south, through some type of bluish force field. I call it a force field because it glows faintly, and it feels like it moves a little when you press on it – so it's not a wall by usual standards, but you can't go through it. On the only open side, my compass says it's west, is a large ornate gate leading into the city. The gate was ajar. I doubt I could have opened it if it weren't. I suppose that was a bit of luck. I can't imagine being stuck on the tarmac for the past week. Maybe I could have climbed the gate or strung some of my clothes together to make a rope.

Through the gate is a walkway. It's surrounded by large buildings on each side. They are crystalline, tall and shining. I haven't found a way to get to any upper levels – the elevator only goes between the ground floor and the basement. From the height of the ceilings on the ground level it may not be that many floors. Either the aliens were very tall, or they really liked high ceilings.

At the end of the walkway is a giant glowing sphere, about fifty feet across. I would guess at one time it had a welcoming message, but it doesn't do anything I can tell, except glow. There's a courtyard north of the sphere through a small, metallic purple gate, and the map chamber to the west. I've been carrying the map I made with me. It's been a week, but I still take a wrong turn every now and then.

There are wide gates out of the city north, west, and south, that lead into the jungle. A footpath hugs the outside wall. Everything beyond the wall is dense jungle. The west and south gates have reception rooms. I think the west reception room is where the Baron set up his quarters. I haven't found any rooms for guests. How can you have a resort without sleeping quarters? Maybe they're on an upper level. Maybe this place was made for daily tours. I haven't found any of the usual amenities of a resort.

The city has an overall damp metal smell. It smells abandoned. I've been to many abandoned buildings on many planets. They usually smell of damp metal. Some smell of decayed plant matter – the primitive ones. The abandoned smell isn't comforting at all. There's a hint of dirt in the areas on the west side of the city. I think it's because they're near the elevator to the basement. There's a southern hall still tracked with dirt from the elevator.

I've been gathering water from the edge of the jungle. When I got off the ship in a hurry, I grabbed my escape bag and a backpack. I have some basic survival gear, plus MRE and those disgusting high calorie bars. I never leave the ship without them in my bag. Well, never since the planet where all they ate were eyeballs. Bird, rodent, frog-like creatures, all eyeballs. They weren't hard to eat. Once in your mouth, they slid right down. No real taste to them at all. Yes, I tried them. I always try the food, but I also bring something with me that won't come back up and say hello later.

I've been sleeping in a jet-black tower to the north. I'm working in the reception room because that's where the Baron left all his papers. I also like the smell of the jungle that comes in through the gate. The jungle smells like life. I couldn't take the lighting in there for sleeping. The tower is dark. If you go to the far corner, away from the portals, you can't see your hand in front of your face. It's probably the best accommodation I've had on any alien planet. Every creature seems to like a little light when they sleep, I don't. The tower is east of a hall with some sort of whispering winds. Honestly, they're kind of soothing. When I'm half-asleep, I can almost make out the words.

Speaking of sleep, that's where I'm heading. Night.

SIGNS OF LIFE

I forgot a sign of life the other night. What was it –
three nights ago? Maybe more. I've been working on the
Osmotic for a few days, but that's not it. I don't think it's
alive. Likely a machine, but it talks. What I didn't mention
are the floating globules in one of the rooms in the
basement. They're evil. They take things from you and
disappear. I don't know what happens to the things they
take.

I've wandered into that room a few times by
mistake. The first time I went in nothing happened. I didn't
have any tools from this planet on me at the time. It was
my 'I just landed, where is everybody?' crazy run through
the buildings. The globules came floating towards me. They

seemed to be checking me out. They look like Earth jellyfish – floating, orange-glowing, jellyfish. I'm not fond of jellyfish, so seeing them floating in the air startled me. I didn't go into the room again until I was making my map, a few days ago. I had tools on me, not many. I'm still matching the tools to the photos and sketches the Baron left. I may have all the level five tools, by the way. Basic tools won't attach to more complex tools and vice versa. I'm exhausting every combination at every level before I move on to the next.

Anyway, so I went in and the globs of stuff started floating towards me, like before, but this time they took my tools. The tools were sucked into them, then both the globules and the tools disappeared in a puff of smoke. I ran out, but it set back my tool making. To be honest, it was mesmerizing. I didn't get out as quickly as I could have. The room adjacent has no globules, but things disappear in there, too. I got a couple branches from the edge of the jungle and put them at the thresholds to the two rooms. They remind me to drop my stuff before I go in, or not go in at all.

I spent the last few day at the Osmotic because it talks and, unlike the gwirg, it's stationary. It's a few buildings over from where I am now – what I call Reception West, or West for short. He's past the Foon-Ball Emporium, through the vacant garden area, and down a covered walkway. I say 'he' because the voice that comes out of it sounds like a man. It's gibberish to me, mostly. Besides the voice, it really isn't at all humanoid, or any alien body form I've ever seen. It's shaped like a hemisphere, mirrored bubble side up, floating a few inches above the floor. The building he's in smells strongly of ozone – fresh, with a hint of Earth geraniums. That a voice comes out of whatever it is makes me feel less alone.

I went there the other morning and sat on the floor. It yelled something in a booming voice, waited, then made a 'bleah' noise. I stayed a while, but nothing else happened. I went out to get something to eat and check my water collecting. I need to find a reliable source for water. This condensation collection system is not going to be enough – plus, I'd like some wash-up water.

After eating (which reminds me I have food for a few months – no more) I went back to the Osmotic. He bellowed, then I repeated the noises he made. Suddenly, he went off in a slew of talk, bellowing on and on. I didn't understand a bit of it, so I simply stood there. After a while, he did the 'bleah' thing again, and nothing more from him. Thinking there may be a trigger at the door, I went out and came back in again. He said that one word he says first, I repeated it, he went through the whole speech again. In frustration I tossed a torkus at him. It went in! Disappeared in the surface. Then, he started a whole new speech, but at the end I caught one word. A tool name. I didn't have it. I couldn't make it. I got the 'bleah'. So, I have to drop things in him. Okay.

I collected a bunch of tools and set them outside the door – in case it mattered. I went in and did the repeat thing and tossed in a gwingus. He said some things I couldn't understand, one word almost sounded like my name, but I recognized the tool he mentioned. He used the same name the Baron had in his notes. More exciting was – I had it. I dashed out, got it, and tossed it in. As soon as it disappeared into the Osmotic there was a thunderous, planet shaking roar. I cupped my hands over my ears and was backing away, preparing to run, but something in the tone sounded like approval – very loud, frightening, approval. Then, a small, black furry creature wiggled out from under the Osmotic. In the gibberish, the last thing the Osmotic roared was 'Zleen', so that's what I've named it.

I really think this thing is alive – Zleen. It has eyes, big black eyes, and a nose and really long, white whiskers. I don't see a mouth though. I poked around where a mouth would be. I couldn't find one, and it didn't bite me. There are no legs on it; no anything but a round furry body with eyes, nose and whiskers. It wiggles across the floor somehow and makes a snuffling sound. It vibrates a little, barely perceptible. It's cute, yes, but thinking about being here a while, I tried to assess whether it was a good food source. It feels like it's all fur. That's both good and bad. Not food, but at least I'm not completely alone.

Exploring the Basement

Setbacks. I hate setbacks. My hair band is gone – the thing the Baron named cacapoo. It slipped out of my hair, and I kicked it by mistake. I was making tools. I didn't mean to kick it, but I did. It exploded into millions of tiny points of light. They fluttered around in the air, then formed two figures – a crystal cube and something like three merged spheres forming a triangle. Sure, I got a clue for making a different tool, but now my hair is all over the place. The humidity is high near the jungle entrances. It's not Florida, Earth in summer bad, but enough to make my hair crazy. The temperature is pretty steady in the building itself. I haven't seen any vents. They may be hidden in the walls.

I decided not to let the cacapoo set me back and not to start breaking things apart to make another. I kept making tools. I have, definitely, all the fifth level devices. Wait, I mean had. That's what I mean.

As I make the tools, I test the tools. The Baron left photos with names, but his notes don't say what the tools do. Some merely have an exclamation point beside the name or on the photo. I was really frightened when I pressed the button on a tool called a rommus. It's a small, beaten-up, black box with a button. I pressed the button and a cable sprung out of it and went straight into my ear. I heard a cry of 'Help!' and the cable retracted. I dropped it immediately. Curiosity got the better of me, and I tried it again. Every press of the button is the same, so I don't think it's something or someone in immediate danger. A few of the other tools have messages, but they are all in the alien language, so I don't understand what they're saying. The rommus must have a translator in the cable.

Some of the tools send telepathic images. Those are interesting, though a bit scary. One is a small, orange, squishy ball the Baron called a rhubarb. I couldn't make out a lot of the message. It's like trying to remember a dream a few minutes after you wake up. You only get glimpses.

The vision was about a room above the jet-black tower. That's where I sleep. There are no stairs, no elevator, no way to climb the walls. The walls are as smooth as glass. I'm hoping it's information I might need and not a warning that a giant, flesh-eating creature lives there. If you're reading this and you can't find me, look for my bones in the tower.

So, I was making the tools, putting them with the photos the Baron left. I had all the level fives. I was pressing buttons like crazy. Listening to weird alien jabber. Watching snuges and mongoos pop out. Having a great time. Then, I got to a tool called a dweezle. It's a hemisphere – these aliens loved hemispheres. I noticed on the back side a little cube attached right in the center, and there was a button. Today was button pushing day, so I pushed it. Everything – EVERYTHING – I'd made imploded. All the tools gone. Poof!

That's when I decided to explore the basement.

The lighted chamber south of West is the elevator. The place I mentioned with the ever reappearing mongoo. It's a portal that appears and disappears with a buzzing hiss sound. Once in it, it flashes bright and dark. Bright is for the main floor. Dark for the basement.

The elevator floor is covered in dirt. I kicked the mongoo. That time I meant it. You can go north or east to get off once you're in the basement. The basement is cool and smells of dirt and glass. You're thinking 'glass doesn't have a smell' but it does. It's a crisp smell. Crisp and clean. It mixes well with the smell of dirt. They're cousins after all. East of the portal is a low passage with the floor encrusted in dirt. North is an equally dirty passage that leads to an observation deck. I honestly wouldn't know if the elevator went up or down, except for the dirt. Dirt means down, right?

I do like the observation deck. It gives me hope there's something more to this place. It overlooks giant crystalline coils. They're beautiful. They are machinery that isn't a game or something that gives you a pet. A short ramp leads east from the deck to the area with the coils.

I was determined not to make any more tools. Not today. I did pop open the box in the far northeast corner of the basement and get a traset. I had found that a few days ago. I don't know how often trasets appear in the box. You can't get one right after another, but they are there frequently. The traset is a bunch of tubes – pale green tubes. I don't know what holds them together. They kind of clank around each other, but don't fall away. The tap sequence will break them apart. They flash and turn into a bork and a bilge. One second pale green cylinders, next a white ball and a green box with a button. The bilge is the green box. It's one of the tools that jabbers on in the alien language. I have no idea what it's saying. The bork is the white ball. I stuck the traset in my pocket.

There are strange lights dancing on the ceiling in one of the rooms; I think it's art. It doesn't take tools. It doesn't acknowledge my presence in any way. The lights dance around in coloured patterns. I've watched them for a while before. They seem completely random.

There's also a room that's filled with a sparkling white mist that tickles my nose. I can't figure out where it comes from. The mist is too thick to see in there. I felt around the walls and floor; there's nothing there. It doesn't have a scent. It has no effect on me, that I can tell. Maybe it was a changing room for the workers?

I didn't bother with the purple, egg-shaped chamber in the northwest corner. It has a slot in the wall, but I haven't figured out what goes in it yet, and this was a non-tool-making day.

There's a dark hall near the elevator with a large machine and a chute. Almost every time I come in the light is out. I can flip the switch and light it up, but I guess it times out after a while. It's a pretty complicated machine, with a chute, pulleys, and conduit. It glows a faint orange colour. It seemed the most promising thing in the basement next to the hopper, but nothing has gone into it. Nothing I've tried, at least. Instead, I went to throw things in the hopper.

The hopper is right across from the coils. Proximity makes me think it runs the coils. The hopper is basically a pale green funnel, merged into the floor at the base. I tried tossing the traset in, no joy. It popped out. Broke it and tried the bilge. It popped right back into my hands. I stopped and thought about the bork, wondering what it might do. No buttons on it, never found a use for it. This time, by thinking about it, I got a telepathic vision. There was a dark subterranean corridor, a set of glowing coils, a large hopper, and a control panel. The number four stood out in my mind, even after the message was over. There I was, standing in front of that same hopper – what does the number four mean? Fourth level tools? Four items go in? I made a note of it but, like most every other telepathic message, I don't know what to do with it, yet.

I threw in the bork. It popped out.. I broke each – because deconstructing tools is not making tools. The bork broke into a torkus and a wigglesnort. Have I mentioned the wigglesnort? It's a coin. A hexagon coin. Why the Baron went with wigglesnort, I can't even guess. I imagine it's for one of the games. I tossed it in the hopper anyway. It popped out. The torkus is a long, cool, rectangular crystal. I tossed the torkus in the hopper.

The coils started humming!

I ran to the next room. They were humming loudly and glowing and I thought 'I am so out of here'. Then, they stopped. I ran around and found another torkus. Dropped it in the hopper. Same thing. Loud, low humming. Coils all glowing. I ran to the room with the console – just north of the hopper – and tried to hit the switch. Still locked in place. The coils stopped humming.

There's an office next to the control room. I curled up on a desk and took a nap. I have a crick in my neck now. The desks are not for sleeping. I'm not even sure they are desks. Not a drawer on them.

Tomorrow, I guess I'll start the tools all over again. It won't be that hard. Some tools make more of the first level items. For example, a dampish – second level – makes mongoos – first level. Once I have those basics tools, I can make the others fairly easily. If I get another traset, I can start pretty well. The traset is third level. The hardest is the nabob. It's a fourth level tool that makes first level gwinguses. I guess I can build around that, or duck out into the jungle a little to pick up a few gwinguses. I'm unsure of the plurals. Would it be gwinguses or gwingii? The Baron only mentions torkii as plural for torkus.

One minute, I'm angry and have sworn off making tools. The next, I'm planning how to make them all again. I need to get off this planet.

SCROOM?

Something woke me a short while ago. I heard a sound – a voice. It seemed to say: 'Beware the scroom!' I don't know what that means. It came from the Hall of Whispers.

I went to sleep with the usual whispering from the hall. Like I said before, it's almost as if I can understand the voices. What woke me wasn't a whisper. I'm sure of it.

Beware the scroom!

I've been digging through the Baron's photos. I found mention of a tool called a scroom. It's one of the sketches where the Baron put an exclamation point after the name. He didn't say what it does. I know what I heard.

It was real. It wasn't alien gibberish. I don't know if this place is adapting to my language, or I'm adapting to it. I need more sleep.

WATER

I have water!

I followed the gwirg again, into the jungle. Of course I got hopelessly lost. I wandered for hours through the palms and ferns. Damp jungle dirt mucking up my boots and weighing me down. The branches almost fight against you, barring your way. There are no paths, no easy ways around. I came to a small clearing and found a half hollowed branch gushing water. I looked around and saw the other end – it's an aqueduct system. I imagine the Baron, or someone else who visited, set it up. It had come apart. I fixed the ends together and followed the system. The end I reached was the source. It led to an area of continuous thunderstorms. I could barely see in front of me for the rain. Glorious rain!

While trying to find my way out of the area with the rain, I came across something else. It's an energy field of some sort, sparkling with sheets of multicolored light within it. It sits inside a little sheltered nook where the rain can't reach it. It floats above the ground about a foot or so and glows gold over the entire exterior. I thought it might be a portal, so I tried to go in it, but couldn't. Watching it glow and spark, listening to the trilling insects, the whistling wind, the fresh smell of the rain outside, I lost track of time. I think I may have napped. When I stood there admiring it, before I left, I declared it the Blub.

I found my way back to the aqueduct and followed it to the city. There, it empties into a cistern buried in the foliage a little ways from the wall. By the time I got there it was overflowing. Water is no longer a concern. Also, all the electronic devices I had with me are now fully charged. I don't know if it was the Blub or something else in the jungle. I may send another video.

LOST AND FOUND

I've explored the jungle. It's been days. When I came back from the Blub I packed up supplies for a few days, grabbed some tools, and filled my pack with water. The next morning I set out. Oh, the things I've found! A landing pad! A derelict spaceship! Monoliths!

I should start with the difficulty of navigating the jungle. The trees and bushes are thickly overgrown with little light coming through. The ground has a constant dampness that scents the air with a richness that almost feels like more smell than your nose can hold. Two hours in I realized my compass was not working properly. Inside the city it seems fine. In the jungle, I would come upon something, a hillock, an unusual rock formation, and head east only to end up back where I'd started. I tried walking *exactly* as the compass pointed, but it wouldn't work. I could walk in what appeared to be a straight line, only to find myself far off from where I expected. They used to say the edge of space loops back around itself. The surface of this planet appears to do the same.

On to the things I found. I first came upon the platform or landing pad. It's a large metal rectangle with a white X in the center. That's why I think it's a landing pad. That, and when I climbed up onto it, I was taken with a vision. There were starships, huge, lined up in berths. Ships of every size and shape imaginable. A small ship veered towards me and landed. I could almost touch it. I tried to stretch out my hand. At least, I think I did. The craft opened and a creature emerged. It had five swaying tentacles coming from its head. It walked with a lumber off the pad and disappeared.

I leaned into the open door of the ship. The console had no controls. The only thing on the smooth interior was a set of numbers – three groups per line, four numbers per group – followed by a cuneiform text. I tried to write them down, but found I couldn't see my arms. I leaned in to get a better look and suddenly felt as though I was falling through space. I awoke on the ground beside the platform. Frustrated, I stepped onto the platform again. The same vision. After several attempts, I realized, though I believe I can clearly see the numbers while in the vision, I cannot remember them once the vision fades – not one number.

The spaceship I found is half-buried in the ground.

It looks like one of those you see in old, fake UFO films. I mean, really! The disc shape and bubble for the pilot. It's almost comical. There's a repeated pattern on the ship in a red fluff material. I couldn't get it open. I tried pulling out tools and pointing them at it – nothing happened.

The best and possibly most important find is the monoliths. They are large and grey. From the vines covering them, they seem to have been here for centuries They have lines of alien language inscribed on them – and numbers. Numbers I could recognize as numbers. I wrote them down. I don't know where to use them. I don't even know if they matter, but they must. They simply must.

The last item I found in the jungle is a mongoosk. I say that is what it is, because that is what it is. It was clear to me as soon as I saw it. I declared, "A mongoosk!" For the uninitiated, a mongoosk is a large thing, not quite plant, not quite animal. Its skin is like that of an Earth rhinoceros or a Blaash sneerz. It has sweenars – large, black spheres – attached to it by flexible silver shafts. Imagine a giant slug with three swaying silver antennae topped with black bowling balls. It was hypnotizing, watching the sweenars sway in the jungle air.

I arrived back at the city more by mistake than intention. With my compass useless, I was simply roaming around and came upon the city wall. I was at the south east corner, though I wasn't sure of it at the time. I walked the small footpath to the south gate, then decided to circle the wall.

The footpath around the wall is well worn. I imagine others would only venture that far once they'd gotten lost a time or two in the jungle. Past the south gate, heading west, I found strange hieroglyphics carved into the wall. To my human eyes, they look like an analog clock or watch, arrows pointing to the center, and a dark sky with a few lights. I will camp out at the edge of the jungle tonight and watch the center of the sky to see if that is their intent.

On the northern wall is a metallic plaque with alien writing. Scrawled under it, in Keplize script, is 'Crack a flungoon open'. I'm not familiar with a flungoon. I couldn't find it in any notes the Baron made. The writing didn't look like his handwriting, though he does know the Keplize language.

Zleen is gone. I left him in the city when I went into the jungle. I didn't have any place to keep him. I told him 'Stay!' several times. I guess he didn't understand me. I searched all the areas on the lower level but can't find him. I did think I saw something wiggling past a doorway, but by the time I got there, he was nowhere to be found.

~ ~ ~

Update: I sat up most of the night at the edge of the city wall, staring at the sky. I didn't see anything special. Stars, two moons, a misty cloud or two floated by in the deep purple sky – nothing out of the ordinary. I don't know what the hieroglyphics mean.

NIGHT IN THE CHAPEL

I have found a second floor. I'm spending the night up here in the chapel.

It started with a wigglesnort in the slot on the main floor. The slot is in the wall near the Hall of Umflungoo. The wigglesnort looks like a coin. It made sense. I dropped it in and a chamber opened in front of me. It was the egg-shaped chamber from the basement – all purple and everything. I went to West, where I'd left the Baron's tool photos, and tried to figure out what might go in the fist-size hole in the wall of the chamber. I found three objects that all have the same alien script on them. They are all a bit egg shaped, like the chamber. I made the tools and went back to the chamber.

The first object I tried was a frakkle. It's smooth like a river pebble. It went into the slot. The slot slowly opened into a portal. I got in and the portal closed, then reopened in the basement. Next, I tried the rukkle – a oblong piece of blue metal. The portal closed and opened on the main floor. That was aggravating. I could do that with no tools using the elevator to the west. There was one tool left. I dropped it in the slot. When the portal opened, I was somewhere I hadn't been before – not ground level, not basement – a second floor!

I would like to say I'm spending the night on this floor to explore it. The truth is, I don't have anything that would work in the elevator to take me down to the first floor. I am hungry. I have only a little water left. I brought a few tools with me, but used them all. Used, probably isn't the best word. Usually when you use something, you get a benefit from it. I did get to watch a video. I watched it several times. There was a lesson in that.

It wasn't all movie watching. There is a laboratory on this floor, with a hopper – a golden hopper. I tried tossing things into it, but they all popped right out. There is also a room with coloured globes. Buttons were pressed, globes did move, but nothing came of it, save a shortly lived light show.

The laboratory with the hopper and globes is down a long corridor, south from the transport portal. At the end of the corridor is a room with a golden desk. A check in spot for the laboratory? The laboratory consists of four rooms, east of the desk. One room has the hopper. One room is entirely gold with a button that looks to be a simple 'start' button and two lights. There's a room with coloured globes, and an adjacent one with coloured buttons that work the globes. I made a quick sketch of the layout and consoles, so I could contemplate them later, then headed off to see what else was around.

At the north end of the long corridor, closer to the portal lobby, is a foyer with wild lights. They swirl and gyrate in multiple colours. They are similar to the lights in the basement, except staring at them made my head hurt. North of the foyer is a small, carpeted room with a Granfalloon. A Granfalloon. The black cylinders wrapping around the dull gold vertical bars. It takes up half the room. I think I gasped when I saw it. Writing this, I'm not sure why.

Granfalloons have a slot so, of course, I pulled out some tools and tried them. Took a few tries before a torrel went in. Out popped a greeb. I need a portable tool chart. I had no idea what it was made of, or what level. It's all glittery with lights showing through its spiral mesh exterior. It was beautiful. I admired it for a minute, then broke it down – wongum, quahog. There are a few quahogs, so I broke that into a dongle and a bagloon. There are several different level bagloons – they all do basically the same thing. You point them at a tool, and they'll replicate it. They remind me of old Earth bazookas, except they're covered in crystalline wires and have two handles, but they do have a sight on them. I should have stopped there and used the bagloon to make some extra tools – I didn't think of it. I put everything back together and made the greeb.

I headed through the doorway to the east, nodding at the Granfalloon on the way out. I don't know why I did that. It seemed right. Like 'Thanks for the greeb'. The area to the east was a bit of a surprise. It looks like a church or a chapel. That's where I am now, where I'll spend the night. It's a long hall with purple metal benches facing the north wall. The north wall is covered in mist right now. There's a persistent hint of incense in the air. The benches are wide enough to sleep on. I was going to sleep on the carpeted floor in the room to the west, but I don't think I could sleep with the Granfalloon watching me.

Heading east to the next chamber I discovered a Ribbenfratz on the north wall there. I swear, I'm not making these names up. I don't know how to explain it. That's what it is, a Ribbenfratz – three tubes coming up from the floor to the red cube, the slot on the side, tubes headed west – Ribbenfratz. I see something new here, and its name pops in my head. If I knew what it did, it would be far more useful. That thought went through my mind, almost as soon as I saw it. It might have been more like 'Curse you, Ribbenfratz, what do you do?'.

I strolled up and dropped in the greeb. I noticed the light in the chapel dimmed, so I ran back in here. What I saw next was magic.

Beware the Scroom

I've seen the old movies of Earth about aliens. I've seen movies aliens make for their own kind. But, I had never seen an alien commercial before. I'm sure that's what it was. I watched it three times. Cost me everything I'd brought with me to make the torrels to get the greebs. I could have used something to snack on.

The wall of the chapel was lit up like a movie screen, so I took a seat. The video started with two misanthropic aliens sitting at a table in what looked like an alien saloon. You've seen the type of place. As soon as you walk through the door, you wonder if you're going to make it out. Maybe you even start backing up, before you run for it. The aliens started arguing. I couldn't make out what they

37

were saying, but I heard the word 'nebbish' and tentacles were slammed on the table. One seemed to be accusing the other of something and, since the nebbish is a tool, I think it was theft.

The argument got heated. They pushed back their chairs and were yelling in each others face. Then one of them slapped a tentacle to his waist. The other looked frightened, started backing up. He took off, then somersaulted, head over, well, tentacles and lost all of his tools. The same tools I've been working with for weeks. They went flying off him in all directions.

Then, it showed the other alien blowing into the end of some tool I haven't made yet – it resembles a gun. He went over and picked up the nebbish, while nearby aliens grabbed the other tools that were blasted off of the thief.

A voice-over started. That's why I think it's a commercial. It was that kind of voice. Blah, blah, blah, alien language and Scroom. Scroom. That's the name I heard from the Hall of Whispers when I was half-asleep – Beware the Scroom. That's the name the Baron had on his drawing. Scroom is a real tool, and that's its real name – not something the Baron made up. He had to be here for at least a month to pick up on the language, the way I've been.

So, the scroom is some type of weapon.

Another clue it was a commercial, the aliens made up as the voice-over spoke. Or, at least, the thief wasn't killed.

Hopefully, this floor works the same as the rest of the planet and, in the morning, new tools will be in place of the ones I took. If not, I don't know how I'll get back to the first floor.

PERMANENT VACATION

I've been taking some time off. I'm on a vacation planet, aren't I? There might not be a spa, but there are games. I have food for a while longer. I have a great shower. Maybe I'll even make my own pool. My change of attitude came after successfully following the gwirg about a week ago.

I'm sure I've mentioned the gwirg, but I don't care enough to look back. It's this silver ball. It floats in the air. It chirps out something – something about the Oolgorboid. I tried following it before and lost it in the jungle. Last week, I was hot on its tail. I followed it like a scrillon on a vexon – hunter and hunted. Whatever it had to show me, I wanted to see. Determination.

I ran over hillocks, through heavy brush, over random tools scattered in the jungle without a second, or first, glance. The gwirg finally reached its destination. It was an Oolgorboid. I could not have been more disappointed. Every day that gwirg flies by, whirring and chirping and tempting me to follow it, and for what? The Oolgorboid looks very much like a large piece of a limp vegetable. I can't eat it. I can't even bite into it – which, I did try. I saw it and slumped to the ground.

I make tools that disappear if I hit the wrong button. I make maps and charts of things with names that come to me, but I don't know what they do – sometimes until it's too late. I still haven't gotten over the dweezle incident. I run through the jungle for what seems hours following a silver sphere, only to be lead to a wilted vegetable?

I don't really blame the gwirg. He's been good company ever since I first got here. Days when I'm working on tools or pressing buttons, or looking through the Baron's notes, he's a nice break. He whirs into a room, and I'll look up.

"Hello, gwirg. How are you today?"

He makes his little announcement and whirs off into the jungle. Sometimes, it's as though he goes out of one door and in another, just to tease me into following him.

He's only doing what he's programmed to do. Can't blame the little guy.

Exhausted from the run through the jungle, and the end result of that expenditure, I decided then and there that I was taking a vacation. I haven't made any tools since. I'm getting pretty good at Umflungoo. Foonball is going to take some work.

Umflungoo is a word game. Alien words, but the alphabet is similar. I started with tool names and guttural sounds, but I think I have it down now. The Hall of Umflungoo is spectacular. It's a large auditorium with colourful banners hanging everywhere. I guess they're the names of previous winners. I wasn't sure it would still work. Looking into the hole in the center of the floor, I saw a large pile of mongoos down below. I took the mongoo from the elevator, didn't even kick him first, brought him back and dropped him in. The west wall lit up. There's an instruction panel on the wall, written in the alien script. Someone had scratched beside it 'Yell Words', so that's what I did. The only words I'm familiar with are the tool names, so I started shouting them out. As I yelled, letters from the words came up on the west wall. You have to guess the word by filling in the blanks on the wall. It felt good to yell.

I didn't win the first few games. The initial game timed out when I left for lunch. I yelled for about a half hour. I walked out a couple other times. The words are foreign. I wasn't even sure I was pronouncing them right. I finally won a game by yelling only letters. Since all the tool names can be written in normal script, I'd yell a letter the way I pronounce it. If that didn't work, I tried a slightly different pronunciation. Finally, I had all the letters on the wall filled. Took me three shouts to say it in a way the game recognized. I won. A shriek went out from the game. The whole auditorium lit up bright orange, something that sounded like trumpets played, and my name was written on the walls, ceiling, and floor in purple lights. My name. This game knew my name. 'Renya wins!' It was intoxicating.

My prize was a flungoon. The flungoon resembles a gold coin, except for the bumps on the surface. I remembered the plaque from outside the city wall. Someone had scrawled 'Crack a flungoon open' under the alien text, so I did. Crackers!

The crackers were a surprise. I'd given up finding anything edible on the planet. Why is there a jungle without fruit? But, there they were. Three unassuming crackers, but the taste! Am I writing to my future self, or are you reading this because you've come to the same fate as I? Have you ever had the after dinner crackers on Banqshaw? That crisp cracker with the goonla spread. That buttery taste so near to cheese. Could be the rationing talking, but these crackers are amazing. Sometimes there are two in the flungoon, sometimes one or three. Three crackers fill me, but I played the game many more times and stored the extras. Forget my high calorie bars; I now always have at least one flungoon on me at all times.

They're all I've eaten for days, and I don't notice any ill effects. If anything, I feel more energetic than I do with MRE. The high calorie bar people should be worried. If I had the recipe, I'd sell them to the known universe.

Foonball is an entirely different game. I've only won once. The Foonball Emporium is a long hall with a holographic figure-eight on the ceiling. Foonball takes a gwingus to play. The gwingus is a silver ball with speckles and a button. Pressing the button makes it wiggle. Besides being one of the primary tools, I've found no use for it, except for making second level tools, and Foonball. I dropped a gwingus in the slot and the game began. The lights dimmed and a ball appeared on the figure-eight.

With no instructions on how to play, I hit the ball. It zoomed along the figure eight. When it came near, I hit it again. There was a honking noise and a light came on above the coin slot in alien script. My name was the first word. The rest, I'm guessing, was something to do with losing. This game also knows my name, but it wasn't nearly as satisfying as winning a flungoon. I played it all day. It was getting depressing. Not only did the game know me, it berated me repeatedly with that honking noise.

After a while, I took to hitting the ball, then watching it. I stopped hitting it every time it flew by, instead hitting it at random times. I finally won. The walls lit up with my name, and a foonprize fell out of the slot. I tried cracking it open, but that didn't work. It's pretty heavy for only about an inch in diameter. The shape is dodecahedron, and it's shining silver. As far as I can tell, it's useless. That hasn't stopped me from playing. I want to master the game. It's good to have goals.

One advantage of the game play is that I can now understand all the messages in the Hall of Whispers. I was passing through the hall one morning and thought I heard something, as usual, but this time I stopped to listen. Though wide awake, I distinctly heard the warning 'Beware the scroom!'. It was as though it were perfect English. I stopped and sat down. The messages came through, faint but understandable. Of them, only two stood out:

"A gwirg is a humanoid's best friend."

"The Granfalloon will often accept a mongoo."

I have only used the torrel in the Granfalloon. If it accepts mongoos, it may give other tools. If it does, there are likely more videos I can watch. Mongoos are readily available. The torrel is a tube, an iridescent mesh over it, a light inside. The mongoo is also a tube, and both feel cold in my hand. I may try other tube-shaped tools in the Granfalloon. It will depend on if I can justify the tool-making while on vacation. Isn't it more like making a ticket to watch a movie?

The gwirg message bothers me the most. Don't get me wrong, I still like the gwirg, but a humanoid's best friend? It runs you through the jungle to be lost, or to find a wilted vegetable. How is that being a best friend?

SOMEONE IS HERE

There is another person here on Beautiful Zurt. His name is Endoon. He's in the Hall of Whispers. I tied him up. He was getting on my nerves.

He got here two days ago. I was on the second level. I had just put a mongoo in the Granfalloon and got out a ravus. I was pretty excited to watch a new movie. As I headed towards the Ribbenfratz, a breeze blew through the room. No big deal, only a breeze, right? I was on the second level. There are no open windows on the second floor. Something was up. I stashed the ravus and made a dash through the rooms. Nothing out of the ordinary, but I couldn't shake the feeling something was different.

I took the portal to the first level and was going to

do the same mad dash. I got as far as the map building when I saw him. He was standing by the wall, looking at the map. He looked over when I came running through the doorway.

"Hello, I'm Endoon. Your map could use repainting." After a few seconds, he looked confused. I realized I was standing there staring at him.

"I'm Renya Zaffor, and that isn't my map." I tried to look casual, loosen up a little.

"So, you're just visiting as well?"

"You could say that."

"It's a beautiful city. How many people live here?" He moved his hand on his tool belt, it was a barely perceivable movement, but adapt travelers recognize it. It was 'friend or foe?'.

A quick glance at the rest of his attire told me everything I needed to know. He was humanoid but not of Earth. I wasn't sure his species. Though I've been to several planets with other humanoid life forms, I couldn't place him. A hint of reptile but larger eyes than most reptile humanoids. His belt held the basic tools of a Collector – the euphemism for looter – rope, a cutting tool, and a weapon of some sort. The weapon wasn't familiar either, except in its basic construct. He wore a black jump suit with extra protection on the knees, elbows, etc. That's their gear for digging through areas they shouldn't be, to take things they shouldn't take, to sell them to people who shouldn't have them.

"You might have thought twice about this planet, but I guess it's too late for that." Wrong thing. I said the wrong thing. Out came the weapon.

"What do you mean?" He looked around me, at the passages out of the map building. He moved to position his back to the wall. The barrel of his weapon trained on me.

"You don't need the weapon. I'm the only one here. And now, you're stuck here with me. If you kill me, you're going to be awfully lonely for a very long time."

"What are you talking about?"

He believed he was in control, with that weapon in his hand. He might have been, but to me, this was my turf. I could run, and if he didn't hit me with the first shot, he'd never find me again. If I made enough noise to help him follow me into the jungle, that would be the end of him. I could probably find my way back. Him? He didn't have a chance.

"I'm guessing your ship is in orbit. It shut down while you were checking out your scans of the planet. You had to teleport down."

"You did that?" His eyes tightened in anger, with a hint of fear.

"No, oh, no. That's what happened when I got here."

"How long have you been here?"

I was waiting for this. If you'd asked me under different circumstances, I would have replied sadly, desolately. With his gun pointed at me, knowing he had come to the same fate, I relished telling him.

"Four months, give or take a few days."

"Why? What's here that keeps you?" He stepped to my left, looking through the doorway again, but always quickly back to me.

"The planet keeps me here. Welcome to Beautiful Zurt. It's your new permanent home."

He reached in his pocket and pulled out his relay, pressed a button, pressed it again. He pressed it several times in a row, each a little more frantic than the last. He looked up, raising the weapon.

"What did you do to my ship?"

"Nothing. The same thing happened to mine. It won't respond. You should have seen it in orbit."

"I saw a ship."

"Did you get a video from the transponder?"

"There was a video. I don't listen to planet promotional drones."

I hadn't thought of that. A lot of planets send out video feeds to passing ships, hoping to lure the occupants in as tourist. I've turned off my receivers before, when passing a known annoying planet. Not only would someone have to come by Beautiful Zurt, but they'd have to have their receivers open. I was crushed.

"You may as well put the gun away. I'm weaponless." I held out my arms.

"What's that on your waist?" He pointed to the ravus I'd stashed in my waistband. I pulled it out. He tightened up.

"It's just a ravus." Two transparent rectangles with a band across them, but I guess the sparkling light inside could make it look like a weapon. I held it out, flat in the palm of my hand.

"What does it do?" He eased up the grip on his weapon.

"I think it plays movies. I'm not sure."

He motioned with the weapon. "Do it. Play a movie."

"I can't do it here. It goes in the Ribbenfratz." I laughed. Maybe, don't laugh at the new guy.

It took about twenty minutes to get him to put the weapon in his belt. Then, the questions started. I thought he might be able to help. After an hour or so more, I realized why he was a Collector. He was dense. He might recognize a shiny Kriyan artifact, but he knew nothing about making tools, testing tools, puzzling out what might be keeping us on the planet, or what might get us off. He wasn't an archaeologist. He was simply a thief.

I tried showing him things. I showed him how to make the tools, how to break them apart. I took him to the different levels. I asked him what he thought about the chute, the hoppers – we even watched the movie the ravus played.

The movie was about making a greeb. I'd already made one, but it was fascinating watching the aliens who invented it putting one together. I could make out more of the voice-over this time. I might have been able to make it all out, except Endoon kept fidgeting around.

"I don't understand anything they're saying. Why are we watching this?"

"Because it might have information we need to get off this planet."

More fidgeting. The only thing that stuck out was a warning not to think about a wongum. I've made that tool before. It was during a tool-making jag. I remember it, because it isn't really substantial, more of a green cloud with sparks. I never thought about its use, luckily. Having seen this video, I'll probably think about it next time I make one. That's how it works. You hear 'don't' and it's all you can do. I'll try to make it in an empty room. Or, maybe I'll give a zarkon II and a felafel to Endoon and have him make one.

The only thing Endoon has shown any interest in is Foonball.

Earlier today I was trying to sort tools by colour,

shape, and other commonalities. It's hard, because there isn't enough space on the floor of one room. I picked out a room for each basic design or colour and was going between them sorting out the tools.

"What are you working on, Renya?"

"Sorting tools. I thought it might help me see a bigger picture. Want to lend a hand?" I looked up. Endoon was eating crackers – pop, pop, pop, down his useless hole of a mouth.

"That doesn't look fun. Want to play some Foonball?"

"No."

"Oh, come on. We have forever, maybe literally, to sort tools."

I glared at him. He didn't get the hint. Ten more minutes of his inane chatter, and I tied him up and put him in the Hall of Whispers. He never saw it coming. I handed him a rommus and pressed the button. The cable came out and went straight into his ear. He didn't even have a chance to see the irony in the 'Help' message. I spun him around and tied his arms, tossing his weapon in with the tools on the floor.

Did he yell? Sure. I let him yell himself out like a crying baby falling to sleep, then I went in and said, "Listen."

"Okay, but let me go first."

"No," I pointed up. "Listen." Then, I went back to work.

He said a few things after that. Things like 'who's talking?' and 'what is this?'. Eventually, he either fell asleep or really is listening to the voices in there. I haven't bothered to check. I hid his weapon in the jungle. He'll never find it, but it might come in handy some day. I was going to drag him out to the jungle and leave him, but I think he might be useful if he adapts to the language.

AN EMPTY MIND

I've been working with Endoon for more than a week now. His time in the Hall of Whispers went better than expected. An empty mind is easily filled. He now knows the language as well, if not better, than I. He's nearly given up Foonball and has joined the search for a way to get off this planet. The only flaw remaining is his zleen. Since he won it from the Osmotic, he hasn't let it out of his sight. He named it Ghost. He's in the basement now. He announced, "Ghost and I are going to look at the hopper." Everything is 'Ghost and I'. They are inseparable.

We've discovered an odd side effect of the tools of Beautiful Zurt. I handed Endoon a tool while working and his appearance changed immediately. He was suddenly dressed flamboyantly and had a small antenna on the top of his head.

"How did you do that?" I asked.

"Do what?" He replied.

"You look different. You have an antenna."

"So did you a minute ago, but now you have a green nostril." He said.

"I what?" That was the best I could do with the information.

I grabbed a bunch of tools and headed to the Osmotic. The surface of the Osmotic is the most mirror-like thing I've found on the planet. I leaned over it and could see my reflection. I had pale lavender skin. I dropped the tool I was holding and looked again. This time I looked very much as I expected, though my hair was a bit wilder than I had imagined. As I shuffled the tools I was carrying, my appearance changed. It was still me, but my hair colour changed, my clothes changed, at one point I was wearing an eye patch.

"So, it's the tools?" Endoon asked.

"Yeah. Why didn't you mention this before?"

"I thought it was a trait of your species. I was trying to figure out if there was some rhyme or reason to it."

I don't know if this is important or not.

We are going into the jungle tomorrow. Well, I am

going with Endoon and Ghost. I will leave my journal here, in case anyone else arrives. If we don't, or can't, return, it may be of some use to the next visitor. Endoon believes the Baron may be in the jungle. I told him I've been out there, and warned him how difficult it is to explore, but he believes he is ready. It makes me feel bad that I haven't fully searched the jungle for the Baron. What if he is out there? What if he was and didn't make it, because I didn't look for him sooner? He is the reason I'm stuck here, but I could have looked harder.

We are taking a tool called the ceeveese. It may be a navigation device. It's a black box, with some spheres and a small screen. On the screen, it always reads the same number in the same area. I've used it at the edge of the jungle, and it doesn't seem to be effected by whatever scrambles my compass. We found out about it in a movie on the second level. Endoon paid far better attention once he'd learned the language. The video was an old one made for tourists. It showed the jungle as a desert, so some type of terraforming has taken place here on Beautiful Zurt. Why they didn't include edible plants makes no sense. The movie also talked about the monoliths. The movie implied there are many more than what I've found. I suppose we will see.

A Snuffle Full of Trouble

It's been two days since my last entry. We didn't go into the jungle. Endoon is now a zleen.

Endoon is a zleen.

I can't get used to this. I don't know how, or if, it can be undone.

I was putting gear into my emergency bag for the jungle when what I thought was Ghost wiggled into the room.

"Renya, snuffle dropped snuffle in snort snuffle! Now snort snuffle snuffle!" The zleen said.

You'd think nothing could stun me anymore on this planet. But there I was, hand halfway in my bag, looking at a talking zleen.

"Ghost?" I asked, finally.

"Snuffle! I snort snuffle!"

The zleen wiggled back and forth in front of me as though it were pacing. It stopped, and looked up at me with its tiny black eyes.

"Snuffle snort!" It declared, and wiggled off.

I tossed my bag on the desk and followed.

I thought it would lead me to Endoon. Instead, it lead me to the chute in the basement. It paced in front of it, snuffling and snorting. It bounced on the floor in front of me.

"What is it, Ghost?"

"Snort am snuffle snuffle!" It said.

"Snort am? I am? Endoon?" Jaw almost to my chest. The zleen, Endoon, bounced and snorted and snuffled, but this time it seemed to be a win. "What happened?"

Endoon, the zleen, wiggled from me to the chute and back again, several times.

"You... put Ghost in there?" Excited bouncing from the ...from Endoon.

If it was to be undone, it would seem putting the

Endoon zleen back in the chute was the way. I crouched down and put out my hands, to make sure we were in the same orbit. He wiggled over and bounced into my arms.

"You're sure?" If a zleen had a head, or wasn't only a head, the movement would have been nodding its head, yes. I dropped him into the chute. He popped right out into my hands. The ground began shaking violently and a deep voice bellowed.

"What zleen is this who dares attempt the infinite loop?" The rumble in the ground fading away with the voice.

"Snuffle!" The Endoon zleen yelled.

"Endoon!" I yelled his name. Nothing. "Ghost!" Still nothing. I looked down at Endoon. He dropped his eyes downward. I set him on the floor.

"I don't know what to do, Endoon. I haven't come across anything about this." He didn't look at me. He simply wiggled out of the room. I went after him.

"I'm sorry. I had no idea that could happen. We'll figure this out."

As much as a small, black ball of fur can, he stopped and abruptly turned around.

"We snort snuffle going snuffle snuffle jungle."

We leave for the jungle in the morning.

In the Jungle, with a Zleen

We're in the jungle. I decided to take my journal with me. I had planned to leave it, when I thought I'd have Endoon to talk to. There's only so much snuffling and snorting a person can take. I know it is still Endoon in that tiny black ball of fluff, but sometimes it's more like having a dog or crenten. It understands you, but you don't understand it. Having anything traveling with me is better than being in the jungle alone, but there's no conversation. This journal seems like more of a real conversation than trying to talk to him.

We've developed a means of communication. It isn't the best, but it helps. Endoon stands – if you can call it standing – a couple feet in front of me. I ask him questions.

If he wiggles towards me, it means yes, away means no. After several attempts, I added wiggling side-to-side as 'I don't know'. Too many answers are 'I don't know'. Like, how can Endoon, in zleen form, carry tools? He wiggles side-to-side in response.

While walking, and wiggling, through the brush I saw Endoon wiggle over a tool. The tool disappeared.

"Endoon, what happened to the tool?"

"Snort have snuffle."

"You picked it up?"

"Snuffle."

"Is that a yes or no?" I said, in frustration.

Endoon wiggled up and gave me a torkus. When he wiggled up, I saw the torkus. It seemed to hover near him, like a caption. I took it and looked at it, then at him.

"How?"

"Snort."

After several conversations almost exactly the same, I came up with the 'yes, no, I don't know' system. I am very glad I brought this journal.

Endoon doesn't know how he picks up the tools. When he's holding something, I can't tell. He can carry quite a few tools, but there's no way to tell he has them. Good thing about traveling with a zleen. I had been carrying all the tools. He also doesn't eat. I kept asking if he was hungry. He would wiggle back – no. Finally, I asked if he has a mouth. I could never find one on my zleen. He wiggled back – no?

"Snort, snuffle snuffle a mouth." He said.

"How can you talk to me, if you don't have a mouth?"

Endoon wiggled side-to-side. I can hear him when he talks. It isn't telepathic like some of the tools. But, if he says he doesn't have a mouth, who am I to object?

The bad part of traveling with a zleen? They don't sleep. Ever. He wants to keep moving, all the time. He gets frustrated with me for needing sleep. The days are long on Beautiful Zurt, longer than my biological clock can handle, but he never needs down time. I drop from exhaustion, only to wake with that furry face near mine, staring at me with those beady eyes. Being in the jungle is a heady enough experience without a zleen staring at me while I sleep.

The ceeveese hasn't been as much help as I'd hoped. It does give the coordinates for your location but, since the jungle is warped somehow, I've had to make a physical map. If I'm at location number 141, I go south and I'm at 142. South again, I'm at 143. South from there, and I'm back at location 141. There's a loop. The ceeveese shows me there's a loop but only after the fact. In places I'll walk east or west, only to find I'm at the same location code, or at a location completely different than the last. A physical map was a necessity.

More than once we traveled for what seemed miles, only to climb a hillock and see the city a short distance away. It doesn't seem as easy to get permanently lost as I'd originally thought. Which doesn't help explain the bones we've come across. Only a few bones, here and there, but many are humanoid. They all look very old, even taking the jungle environment into account. I don't know if they ran out of food or water, but it looks like there were a few travelers who never made it off the planet. The first bones we came across shook me. When we saw more, I thought it would completely unnerve me. All I found was more determination. That will not be me. I will not end up a pile of dark bones on a planet miles from anywhere I'd consider calling home.

We've come across a few things I saw on my previous journeys out here. Endoon didn't seem impressed with the platform. When I found it, I must have stood on it and watched the vision it produces three times, at least. Once was enough for him, and he was ready to move on. I asked if he knows more about the planet in zleen form. He wiggled back – no.

We followed the gwirg to the Oolgorboid. Humanoid running. Zleen wiggling. Finally reaching it, with me out of breath and no sign of distress from Endoon. If a zleen can laugh, I think that's what he was doing. When I first saw it, months ago, I almost lost all hope. He wiggles around with a chirping noise. Limp vegetable – hilarious!

We took our time leaving the Oolgorboid, going back to mapping our movements. The monoliths are all around the area. We found seven! I don't know how I missed the others on my first trip to the Oolgorboid. Each monolith is a large grey rock, jutting out of the rich jungle floor. Vines cover them, but under the vines are coordinates. I can read the alien script now. Seven monoliths, seven coordinates. I don't know the final destination of the coordinates, but they aren't the same ones that got me to this planet. One of the monoliths has an extra notation: Next exit, 49 miles. To the best of my calculations, that would be somewhere in the city. It's hard to tell with the warping of terrain in the jungle, so I can't be certain. If it is right, we've covered a lot of ground in the time we've been out.

I have to sleep. I have to. I asked Endoon not to watch me sleeping. As I lay down, he wiggled off. I was going to call after him, ask him where he was going, but realized whatever he replied would only be a snort or a snuffle.

THE BARON HAS BEEN HERE

I found a recorder that I'm sure is the Baron's. We climbed to the top of a mesa and were admiring the view, when I saw a glint of light near the edge. It's a small TR7 personal recorder with the initials BTH engraved on it. I don't know if there's anything on it. The power is drained, and it has a device specific battery pack. Some vintage style I haven't come across before.

The climb up the mesa was hard, for me at least. Endoon climbed almost straight up. I had to search for footholds and solid grips. Finding a mesa in the middle of the jungle calls attention to the planet once being desert land. From the top of the mesa you can see the vastness of the jungle, slightly more blue than green, because of the bluer sun.

In the distance – I would call it west if west existed in the jungle – I could see the shimmer of the city. If the Baron made it to the top of this mesa, he should have been able to make his way back. Endoon and I will try going west, to see if there is any other trace of him.

I've been thinking about the Baron since we found the recorder. Every time I traveled with him, we always visited inhabited planets. Only once did we transport to an abandoned planet, and he wanted to leave right away. That's why we parted ways. I wanted to explore ancient alien civilizations. He wanted to make friends with every species in the universe. I think he needs an audience. There's no audience here on Beautiful Zurt. I can't imagine how he could survive without one. Maybe the word survive is wrong. He always proved himself to be resourceful. His survival would seem very possible, physically. I don't know how he would cope with being alone. He might have sent for me, not out of some sort of malice or even to teach me a lesson, but because he couldn't stand being alone. Who could he talk into coming into a really bad situation, because he needed someone to talk to, along with some help? In his list of contacts, I imagine I rank among the highest in gullibility.

Endoon has agreed to head west but doesn't want to go back to the city. Whether we find something or not, he wants to continue on. It almost seems like he objects to going back to the city at all. Maybe zleens are jungle creatures by nature. It would explain why my zleen left the city. Maybe being a zleen-humanoid is only temporary, and he'll wake one day all zleen.

I have learned zleens, or maybe just Endoon, cannot be trusted. I still wake to his furry face staring at me. Every morning. I don't know if he spends the whole night staring at me or appears before I awake. Every night, he heads off into the jungle, but there he is every morning. I ask him if he found anything. He always answers no.

EAST, NOW NORTH

We believe we've explored the east and north completely. The furthest point north is the Blub. That's where we are now. Or, I am. Endoon wiggled off somewhere, because I'm bedding down here for the night. Endoon likes the Blub, from what I could tell. He spun and wiggled in front of it when he saw it.

"What are you doing?" I still talk to him as though he can answer.

"Snort snuffle snuffle Blub!"

"I know it is. Do you know if it's important?"

"Snuffle snort be!"

"What?"

He wiggled up to me, then back a few paces and stopped. It took me a minute to get the hint.

"Do you know if it's important?" I asked again. He wiggled backwards. "Do you think it might be?" He wiggled side-to-side. "Then, why are you so excited?" He stared at me with his tiny, beady eyes. I had forgotten the syntax. "Are you just excited to find it?" He wiggled forward.

Conversation is so difficult with a zleen – well, a zleen humanoid. My zleen never spoke.

We didn't find any other evidence that the Baron had been in the area. Not a footprint or a bent branch. We did find another monolith. It had a poem engraved on it. The main part was 'statues always tell the truth, heed them for eternal youth'. I don't have any idea what that means. I haven't seen any statues and, while eternal youth sounds great, I'd rather have it tell me statues will get me back to my ship and out of this whole planetary system.

It's been almost six months since I first arrived. It hasn't been all bad, but I was ready to go months ago. Six months is the most I've spent on any planet. It was an archaeological dig on Jefrond 5. It had been centuries since any living creature had visited the planet. The lush overgrowth was not unlike the jungle here on Beautiful Zurt. The main difference is the insects. While I've seen none on Beautiful Zurt, though I have heard buzzing, they were deadly on Jefrond 5. They were enormous, twice the size of an average human, and looked like a mix between an Earth dragonfly and a mosquito. That isn't too hard to imagine, but imagine the most beautiful dragonfly you've ever seen mixed with the most horrible biting mosquito. The team I was working with called them Sykils.

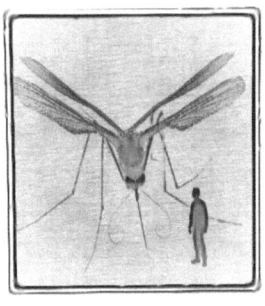

Their beauty was how they'd get you. They shimmered and threw off colours in the sun. You stand still for one second to admire them and half your bodily fluids are gone. One Sykil would put on a show, while the others would sneak up behind you and suck out your juices. Prior to my arrival the team had developed special suits the Sykil couldn't penetrate. They lost six team members testing materials they were sure would work. Once the Sykil realized they couldn't bite us, they started taking our supplies. Vicious, and spiteful. 'Tie it down or lose it!' Brenner, the leader, would shout every night before we bedded down. I once watched a group of Sykils carry off a small vehicle.

The artifacts on Jefrond 5 were amazing. You knew they had to be, that anyone would brave the planet. Silicon vessels they used for cooking. Silicon walls for their homes. Everything had bold geometric patterns carved into them, the grey accented with a red paint made from rocks in the area. A meteor strike had killed off the planet, so we mostly found pieces – thousands and thousands of pieces. We never found a body, or a grave, or any monument with a depiction of the race who once lived there but, from planets in the general area, the assumption was those who left had colonized elsewhere. One of the closest planets had stories of coming from the stars. They had been passed down in the oral history.

I was going to say I miss exploring, but I am exploring. How can you miss something you're currently doing? Maybe I'm just sick of Beautiful Zurt?

I don't think that's it. It really isn't a bad planet. It could use an adequate water system, but water is available. There's an area of constant storms right outside this nook with the Blub. It could use guest rooms with beds, but I've slept on worse jungle floors than here. I've slept in caves with water dripping on me all night. It could use music. I haven't heard music since I got here. That's not entirely true. I have thousands of songs on my mobile com, but I've only allowed myself to play a little bit here and there. With no reliable source of power, I have to reserve what I have. My ears have to be very hungry for me to give up power for a piece of a song.

It isn't that I hate being here. It's more about not having a choice. If I knew I could leave tomorrow, well, I would. But, if I'd known from the day I landed that I could leave at any time, I think I might still be here.

I'm ready to head back to the city. In a small way, it's like being homesick. I miss my jet-black tower. I miss the shimmer of the portals. I miss the smell of the basement and popping a traset out of the box there – even when I don't need one. I have a map of the areas we've been. I've gathered enough information to keep me busy for a while, and I don't want so much it's a burden to go through. Some of the tools may go into the Blub or the Oolgorboid. Everything we've brought with us failed, as well as everything we made along the way. I didn't bring a tool chart, but I did note what we tried. I need to bust into the Baron's recorder and see if I can wire it up to another power supply. I have work to do that I can't get done here. I need to be in the city.

A MESSAGE FROM THE BARON

It took several days, but I'm back in the city. Endoon isn't with me. He said he wanted to continue exploring. At least, he answered yes to questions that led me to that conclusion. I don't expect to see him again.

I listened to the Baron's recording. It was more than I'd hoped for. First, I didn't have to do any wiring or rigging to get the recorder going. When I took it out of my pack, it was fully charged. It's the Blub. I'm sure now. Everything I took with me is fully charged, even the backup batteries that were rolling around in the bottom of my pack. I will have music but, of course, the Baron's recording took precedence.

I've listened to the recording over and over. I was

surprised how good it was to hear the Baron's voice. I half expected the voice of a friend reaching out across time to tell me they understand where I am and what I'm going through, maybe even an apology. But, of course, we are talking about the Baron. He's never been big on sentimentality. Plus, it's his fault I'm here, but it's still good to hear his voice. I'm sure he left the recording for me, but he doesn't address me directly. I guess, in case I never made it here, or never found it.

"Dear Fellow Traveler! I hope you're enjoying your stay on Beautiful Zurt! The amenities are not as you may have expected –he's talking to me here, admitting he tricked me– *however, the shining city and expansive jungle should make up for minor inconveniences."*

Minor inconveniences? King of understatement, my friend the Baron. He goes on about the beauty of the city. The fun of the games. The new and exciting discoveries around every corner. He's got me there. Every point is true. As I said, if teleporting off had always been an option, I may have stayed on my own.

"If you are finding this recording, you know by now what you must do. You must solve the puzzle that is Beautiful Zurt. You must pave the way for others to come and go from this planet as they please. And, they will come. They will come and play and explore this wonderful planet. Our planet, Beautiful Zurt."

Our planet. Am I being naive thinking this was meant for me? Am I being gullible? Even in a recording, the

Baron knows how to inspire, motivate, flatter a person into doing what he thinks needs to be done. This is exactly what I've seen him do with every species we've met from a two foot Parsoniz to the ten foot Creaon. One minute we have weapons drawn on us, the next we're honored guests. Why should the charisma that works on every race in the known universe not work on me?

~ ~ ~

I was playing the recording again and stopped to write the last paragraph, but forgot to turn the recording off. I read what I wrote and thought about how he may not have meant it for me and, if he did, wasn't he simply trying to get me to do what he wanted? Then again, maybe all he wanted was help? After several minutes of jungle winds and shifting clothes, the Baron's voice came on again. It was low. He hadn't realized he forgot to hit stop.

"Curse it all. I hope you find this, Renya." Then, a shuffling noise as though he were walking and, after some time, a click.

I've found it Baron, and I will find you, too.

How I Met the Baron

Baron Tarris Hylke is not without his secrets. I didn't hear his full name until I'd known him some six months. I don't think he's really a Baron. He may be a madman. I call him Baron anyway. I traveled with him for almost three year, back when I was starting out.

We first met in a canteen on the Foxx7 outpost. I had learned the game of Glackow, because I heard it was a good way to make contacts. It's a very complicated game of dice and cards. It's only played by the old-timers, and those who've worked closely with them. I wanted to explore. I wanted it more than anything. I wanted access to rare and unexplored worlds. That information is the kind of thing the old-timers keep close. A little known planet might be a great place to set up a homestead for your retirement from space. A little explored planet might hold riches you haven't had time to look for, yet.

I was playing a table of old-timers, and I was doing okay. You should never win too much, or lose too much. It's a fine balance, and if you tilt to either side people tend to get suspicious. I dropped out of a hand, a courtesy move after you win a big pot. Lots of new players don't understand that rule, and it can mean trouble if you don't. Glackow is not a game of greed. I wandered over to the bar for a fresh drink.

"You're very good at Glack." The Baron had walked up to the bar next to me. He rested his elbows on the bar, grasping his glass in both hands.

"Thank you. Do you play?" I tried to size him up. He was a stout man, older, bearded, a chest filled with regalia from places I'd never seen. You'd think ex-military, except he wore an animal skin hat, furry greys that almost matched his beard.

"A little. I can see you've studied the game extensively. However, you could use some work on your slap-fold." He had my attention. Every aspect of the game was exacting, having developed over years of space travel when a haul took three times or more what they take now.

He turned around to face the table of players and

dipped his head in a conspiratorial manner.

"You slap the cards well, but try giving a subtle sigh as they hit. Old-timers love to hear that sigh. It's almost better than whatever is in the pot."

As soon as he said it, I realized I'd heard it throughout the game from other players and hadn't pick up on it. I kicked myself for not catching it.

"I'm Renya Zaffor." I offered my hand. He looked at it, then extended his own.

"You can call me, The Baron. From Earth?"

"Yes, I – how did you know?"

"Handshaking is mostly an Earth custom. You can tell a lot about a person by their greeting. How long have you been out?"

I confessed I was green. He didn't hold it against me. We talked through the night. Mostly the Baron talked, regaling me with stories and offering advice. I would have sworn he was a long lost uncle who was sent to look after me, but there wasn't anyone back home to send him. I have no family on Earth, that's what drew me into space. I had just finished a gig with some archaeologists. The Baron asked if I wanted to ride along with him until I saved up enough for my own ship. It was the biggest, and up until then the only, lucky break I ever got.

I came into space as a volunteer on an archaeological dig. I didn't have a background in archaeology, but I had worked hard to get a small vessel pilot's license. Lots of people know how to dig, not so many can pilot a collector across a planet or back to the main ship. I couldn't afford a ship of my own. I could barely afford the basic equipment required to volunteer. Everything came from surplus stores and resellers. The tent I took with me had a hole in the roof. I didn't know that until I unpacked it and set it up, light years from any supply station.

The Baron taught me a lifetime's worth of information on exploring space. I'm not sure he meant to teach me everything he did. Some of it he taught me only because he loved to talk, and I never underestimated the value of his knowledge. I always kept in my mind that I'd missed the slap-fold sigh. The Baron, watching from tables away, had spotted my omission.

I learned how to greet different races in their own way, or the way of their nearest ally. With some species using their own greeting would be insulting, too familiar. The most surprising thing the Baron taught me was also one of the most simple. Almost any race, on any planet, will respond to you in a friendly way if you tell them you are lost. Sure, there are a few out there that will make you the main course for a lost traveler luau. The Baron had a stellar map with three such planets marked. He had me add the coordinates to my com with an alarm if I came within their general area. He didn't say how he found them; he didn't seem to want to talk about it. One thing about the Baron, since he loves talking, if there's something he doesn't talk about, I never asked. Not really never. I tried once to ask if he had any family. He said, "Isn't important," in a way that let me know not to push. The Baron has his personal secrets, and he doesn't give them up.

WHAT DO YOU DO WITH A REBOZO?

One of my favourite things to drink is Candar Cola. Sure, there's no cola in it. They call it that to appeal to Earthers. I have some on my ship. If my ship's still out there. I keep them in the chiller. Nonce, I could use one right now. I shouldn't think about it. I had a point.

Imagine your favourite drink. You go to your chiller and pull one out. The cold bottle in your hand lights up your brain. Like Pavlov's dog, you know what's coming. You flip back the stop and tilt it into your mouth. Glorious.

Now imagine you pull out that bottle, flip the stop, tilt it back and syrup comes out. Thick, gooey syrup, instead of your favourite beverage. My syrup is something called a rebozo.

Since I started making tools, months ago, I always get a traset out of the box when I'm in the basement. Even when I don't need it, I find myself popping one out and taking it. I've probably described the traset before – faded green cylinders that clank around each other but don't come lose. I'm not sure why I like it. Maybe it's the clank, clank sound it makes. Maybe it's because, early on, a traset was a good start for building more complex tools. I was in the basement this morning and popped the box open. A traset didn't come out.

All the hundreds of times I opened the box, out came a traset. Today, for no reason I can think of, a rebozo came out. It's sitting beside me, beeping softly. It looks like two round dinner plates attached face to face along the rims – a little puffy in the center, a little heavy on one side. The edge is sharp – not sharp enough to be a weapon, unless you were really close and really strong. I don't understand how it got in the box. I've never seen it before. It's not in any of the tool notes the Baron left. It doesn't break apart or attach to anything else. I don't know what it does. I've tried thinking about it – nothing.

Thinking about a tool is always my last resort. Some tools, you think about them and they do things. Take the wongum, mentioned in the movie, I did eventually make one – in a room, alone – and think about it. Nothing happened. I didn't have any tools on me, so I went out and picked up a few first level items. Thought about it again.

Nothing. About a minute later, one of the tools I was carrying disappeared. Okay, I thought, so it makes a tool disappear. Another minute later, another tool disappeared. I broke the wongum down to a felafel and a zarkon II. In categorizing, I've classed it as a weapon. Much like the way I used the rommus to distract Endoon to tie him up, I could use the wongum to disarm someone. It would take time, but they may not figure out what was going on.

There's a green cylinder in the jungle. It's about a foot across and buried in the ground. I tried digging it up but can't. Maybe it's part of some duct system. I put the rebozo in there, with a foonprize and Endoon's gun. They are all the things that don't seem to have a purpose here. At least, none that I've found.

~ ~ ~

I went down to the box in the basement a minute ago. A traset came out. All is right with the world.

Endoon Returns

Endoon and I are in the jungle again. I'm not sure how much of Endoon is left in the zleen, but he came to the city wanting me to follow him into the jungle. I haven't been able to find out why. Yes, no, and I don't know, doesn't work when you can't ask the question properly because you don't know even the general topic. I got as far as 'Did you find something?'. To that he answered yes. Where do I go from there? I can't ask what it is. I tried. I got a string of snorts and snuffles. I can't guess what it is anymore than I could have guessed a rebozo would one day come out of the box in basement.

When he showed up outside the door of West, I was surprised. When he wouldn't come in the building, I realized whatever he wants me to see, I should see now, while it still matters to him. We left through the west reception area and followed the wall to the southwest corner. We stayed on the path, around the wall and past the south reception door. Then we headed east, but he's been leading me south for the past few hours. It's what I call south, but the ceevees is going crazy with the location numbers. Sometimes, we go back a bit, and forward again. I hope he knows where's he's going. We've been walking all day and some time into the night. He wanted to keep going, but it's dark, I'm tired, and I'm not a tiny ball of fluff that can get through the branches and brush with ease — especially in the dark.

THE ORB

A thousand years I've waited

I'll wait a thousand more

Rebozo's sweet caress, you know

Is power, to the core.

It was worth the journey. There is a giant orb on a pedestal in the middle of the jungle. It must be twenty feet across, pale and translucent. It looks similar to the orb in the city – the one that only glows and nothing else. I wasn't expecting much when I saw it. As soon as we came into the clearing, Endoon started his wiggle-in-joy dance. Then, he wiggled at top speed up to the orb and along the vines wrapping its base. When he reached the orb, he brushed against it, the way animals scratch themselves on trees. The orb began to glow and swirl and Endoon went flying. A column of red appeared in the center of the orb. I was ready to run to Endoon when a voice came rumbling from the orb. It was more sound than words. Above, is what it said.

Rebozo.

It was worth waking up this morning with those beady eyes staring at me. I don't know what it means by core. Perhaps, it's some central computer that keeps the city lit and cool. Maybe it's the core of the transport system. I asked Endoon when he found it – was it a day ago? Two days? He found it the same day I found the rebozo in the box. His presence at the orb somehow created a rebozo in the city. This is new.

Endoon barely gave me a second to take it all in, and he was headed off again. I wanted to map it out. I wanted to be sure I'd be able to get there again, if I needed. I didn't have a chance. He slides under fallen branches with ease, and I have to figure out if I can go over or around them. I called out a few times for him to slow down. All I got was a snort or a snuffle.

At the end of a long run, we made it to a monolith. I was disappointed. I expected something unusual or exotic, like the orb, but it was only another monolith. I walked around it, pulled at the vines, and realized it was *different* monolith. It had a coordinate we hadn't seen before. That makes eight numbers. Eight numbers and the order they go in. Eight isn't enough for a location, but it's one digit closer than seven.

Endoon said he's going off to look for more. He told me how to get back.

"Did you find more?" He wiggled back.

"Are we going back to the city?"

"Snort are." He said.

"We are?" I asked. He wiggled back.

"You're staying here, aren't you?" He wiggled forward.

"How will I get back?"

Endoon headed in one direction, not forward, not backward, not side-to-side. I followed.

"This way?" He stopped and stood still for a second, then wiggled towards me.

I'm going to sleep now. He's left already. In the morning I'll head in the direction he told me and hope for the best.

A Toast to the Statues

It's been a few days, maybe a week. I was in the jungle for a while. When I got to the city wall, I decided to head west. Well, west by my reckoning. I tried south first, but I wasn't going anywhere. The ceeveese kept reading the same number, no matter how far I walked. I headed north, and the city wall suddenly appeared in front of me. I decided to try west. I didn't get very far. There's a tight loop at the edge of the city to the southwest corner. Finally, going a little west I was able to go south. I think.

If the numbers on the ceeveese change, I must be making progress, right?

I found new, exciting things. The statues are probably the most impressive discovery. They're huge, at least twenty feet tall, and made of some type of jet black, smooth stone – the same as the walls of the tower where I sleep. They may be the original occupants of Beautiful Zurt. They remind me of the Earth Buddha. Their braided tentacles. Their contemplative look. The foliage draped around them only adds to the mystic.

Each statue – there were four total – has a different poem they chant. More of a riddle than a poem. They are all very similar in appearance, except for the amount of jungle that's covering them, and each has a distinctive voice. One booms its riddle. Another has a grinding voice. Perhaps they represent famous aliens who once ruled here. I thought they were only monuments, but I've developed a habit of talking to myself. Months with no company, little company, and a zleen-human can have that effect. I found two statues and was at the second, looking at my hand-drawn map, and started talking to myself. My voice must have triggered the statue. It started its riddle with a droning noise, barely distinguishable as speech. It took me a while to realize what was happening.

After the second statue talked, I went back to the first. I did everything I'd done at the second, walking around it, pulling off some vines, rubbed it to feel the smooth stone surface. Nothing happened. Then, I asked aloud, "Why does the other one talk?" Its low rumbling voice started. As I found more, I'd simply say 'Talk to me, statue'. I had to hear each riddle a few times to write them down. I may have all the coordinates to get out of here. That is, if I ever find something that will take them.

What else did I find? What more? I found a Freenish. It was yet another case of 'I know what it is, but not what it does' until it does what it does. A Freenish is a large complicated machine with parts jutting off at odd angles. One of the tubes on it comes down the front to form a spout. Its gold sides shone in the sunlight. It's the first working machine I've found in the jungle. I don't consider the orb a machine. It's more of a relic, like the statues. The Freenish is a giant percolator for a pale blue liquid. It's not Candar Cola, but watching the liquid bubble up inside brought on an awful thirst.

I was sitting on the jungle floor watching the liquid dance around inside the Freenish when I saw a drop come from the spout. It was a tiny drop, and it disappeared as soon as it hit the ground. I moved closer just as the spout started gushing the sparkling blue fluid, and you know what? I drank it. Hindsight says that probably wasn't the smartest thing to do. I did it anyway. It's the first thing that isn't rainwater I've had since I got here. It was delicious, a little tart, and filled with tiny bubbles that tickled my throat all the way down.

Was it safe? Define safe.

I'd been in the jungle days. I'd seen a swirling orb. I'd seen giant talking statues. So, yeah, I drank from the Freenish. I didn't feel any ill effects, for about three minutes. I wouldn't really call it an ill effect. In any canteen, on any planet, people pay good money for that effect. Nonce, did I hallucinate.

It started with vertigo, then my whole field of vision was taken up with images in a microscopic view – tiny things darting about. That expanded up to dancing aliens and cubes and colours and – it was bizarre. Thing is, it didn't hit me all at once. I felt a little light-headed right after I drank from it, but that passed quickly. I was walking off to explore some more when the first vision hit. Stunned me off my feet. I dropped down and experienced it in all its glorious weirdness. When it was over, I got up ready to move on. I only traveled a short distance when I was hit again. I'm not sure if I sat down or fell down that time, but when it was over I was on the ground. That's when I decided to head back to the city. The third hallucination hit a few minutes later. Then another as I reached the south gate of the city. I haven't had any more since. I'd like to say I won't do that again, but I probably will. The Freenish juice tastes amazing, and now that I know what happens, it won't be so bad next time. I hope.

ONE YEAR ON BEAUTIFUL ZURT

I haven't written in this journal for a while. I've had my head in notes, charts, maps. There is some progress, however, so I thought I should make note of it.

I have activated the button in the basement. Since a torkus was the tool that went into the hopper and made the coils hum, I examined similar tools. Trying them in different orders, I've been successful in making the button on the console push in. The effect lasted a while, then the button returned to the off and locked position. I am bookmarking this page with the list of tools and the order. I'm considering this step one. I don't know how many steps there may be, in the end.

[ed. The bookmark is not with the papers]

The bookmark also has colours listed. Those are the order of the globes on the second level. They must be brought down in that order to turn on the light on the gold console. I spent a week on the second level trying different colour orders. There is still the question of the gold hopper. The globes make one light on the console light up, but I can't find anything to go into the gold hopper to light the other. The suvar has a gold stripe on it. It creates wigglesnorts. The narret is a large gold sphere. It has a message that's a little unnerving, like overhearing aliens talking about you. Neither of them worked. There is gold on several of the machines – including the Freenish and the Blub.

Speaking of the Blub, I've been going out to recharge my electronics about twice a month. I usually stay overnight in the nook. The Blub is bright – a gold corona with multicoloured lights swirling below the surface – but the trilling insects and the whistling winds make up for the light. The sounds drone me to sleep quickly. It's like a vacation home. It's how I get away from the city for a few days.

I'm afraid I'm settling into patterns. I don't think I've become discouraged. I've been trying things. Every day I try new things. The solitude is getting to me. I haven't seen Endoon in months. Becoming a zleen isn't the worst fate. I was out in the jungle for a couple weeks and came back to a pile of ash in the center of the floor in the map building. It was a large pile of ash – and a shoe. Either someone spontaneously combusted when they hit the planet, or they realized the situation and took the cowards way out. All my notes, drawings, photos, scattered over the desk weren't enough to convince them there was hope. I scooped up the ash and threw the shoe as hard as I could into the jungle. I don't want to dwell on it.

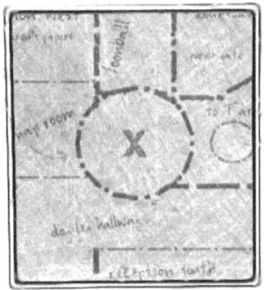

The days seem to run together. Not always, but for days at a time. I only realized I hadn't made any journal entries in months when I checked my com and saw that it's been a year since I teleported down to Beautiful Zurt.

My weeks in the jungle gave me two new discoveries, a Nofzinger and a Oddlewokkus. They seem related to the Blub, in nature and in distance from the city. The Blub is very powerful. The Nofzinger and the Oddlewokkus must be as well. They are the three furthest things from the city.

A few weeks ago I discovered something new in the domed building north of West. The ceiling is covered in tiny coloured lights. I was in there examining the lip around the edge of the floor. I thought I might be able to see it better if all the lights were blue. The lights on the ceiling flickered when I had the thought. I thought of them being blue again – flickering. I went through colours, thinking each colour in turn. When I thought green, all the lights changed to green. The more I thought green, the brighter they got. Is it important? I don't know.

A year. What do I have to show for a year of trying to leave this planet? A year of not finding the Baron.

When I first got here, and for a while after, I was sure the Baron was somewhere on this planet. I'm not so sure anymore. But, if he isn't, does that mean he found a way to get off? From the notes he left, I don't see how that's possible. There are things I discovered for which he made no note. The Freenish isn't in his notes. The movies aren't in his notes. Did he even make it to the second floor? With the gold rooms and hopper in the laboratory, I can't believe that wouldn't be necessary to leave. Did he find a secret way out? He could never be the ash person. Though he is many things, a coward is not one of them.

LEAPS AND BOUNDS

I have, in my possession, an Oolgorboid. I can't believe I actually have one. A free Oolgorboid!

It's taken me two months of jungle excursions but I am now sure, completely sure, I have seen everything in the jungle. I have created objects that don't break apart into other objects, by tossing tools into the Blub, Oddlewokkus and Nofzinger. I am not sure what they do, nothing that I've seen yet, but I have them. The best thing, or what excited me the most, was freeing the Oolgorboid.

Yes, I'm sure I told you the Oolgorboid resembles a limp vegetable, but it was not obvious or easy to free it. The only reason I tried was because of the gwirg. Why would the gwirg continue trying to lead me to something that doesn't matter? The Hall of Whispers says the gwirg is a humanoid's best friend. You put those two things together and it equals the Oolgorboid is important. I tried tossing devices into it, pulling it out of the ground, cutting it off at the base, pointing every gun-like tool at it, thinking about it – all the usual things the aliens seem to have done with their devices. No gun device worked, so I moved on to others. Finally, I pointed a tool at it, and the Oolgorboid began to writhe, then it emitted an ear-piercing screech and fell free from the ground.

I've gotten pretty good at breaking down and reconstructing the tools. I haven't seen my tool chart in months. Months. I haven't used a ceeveese in the jungle in... I can't remember the last time. Even though the jungle will not be beaten down – I've never gone out and seen where I had walked the previous day – I can find my way by instinct and the stationary relics scattered there. Freenish? West.

I did drink more from the Freenish. But it was research. The Freenish juice cannot be carried away from it. The second it touches anything, besides my mouth, it evaporates. I'd have to set up camp near it, if I had a problem. I usually stop on the way back from the Nofzinger for a drink. The visions are about aliens dancing in cubes. It's always the same four images, but every time I can remember a bit more of the details.

I've taken all the non-tools – things that won't break apart – and put them with the rebozo and Endoon's gun in the cylinder, except for the Oolgorboid. That, I keep with me. I thought it was the only one on the whole planet, but the gwirg kept coming by asking me to follow it. I gave in and followed the gwirg a few weeks after I had freed my Oolgorboid. There was another in its place. I am still keeping mine. It is my Oolgorboid.

One thing I did not see in all my adventures into the jungle is Endoon. I have heard the brush rustle nearby, but never find anything when I investigate. Sometimes, while sleeping at the Blub, I've dreamt I awoke in the night with those beady black eyes staring at me. I'm sure it's only a dream. I've never woken completely to find him there. I never see the insects I hear buzzing either. It's almost as though they're on the other side of whatever loops space in the jungle.

My next move is trying all the non-breakables in the golden hopper. Something has to work in there. Maybe I'll take in a movie while I'm up there. I could use a break.

IMAGES AND VISIONS

The Freenish vision got me thinking. What if some of the easily dismissible visions from some of the tools are actually very important? I had to dig out my tool chart to explore this idea. Though I know how to use about eighty percent of the tools, and can make all of them from memory, I don't remember all the visions the tools give. Take the cacapoo I use as hair bands. If I took out the one in my hair right now and kicked it, I would have a vision of how to build a nebbish. Many of the visions are like that. Some are ads, complete with the name of the company that invented the tool – a few are more esoteric. On my tool chart, I've noted which tools give visions, and which visions are tool instructions or advertisements. Some have the 'v' for vision but aren't marked with a tool name they describe. Those are the ones I decided to investigate.

Take for example the bundle. The bundle is small metal box. It has a wire hanging out on one side and a switch in the other. If you flip the switch, you get a vision of a curved surface with millions of tiny lights. This sounds like the domed building. Then, it shows a console with four lights. I've never seen a console with four lights. I've found two consoles with lights – each by a hopper. Somewhere, there must be another console. I thought I'd found every room and building in the city. There must be an area I haven't found yet.

The narret is a large, heavy, golden sphere. Its message is disturbing. It feels as though your head splits

open and the thoughts of alien creatures fill the crack. One of the things you overhear is the tools that make a snaack – not a snack like the crackers, but a tool called a snaack. The other thing you overhear is them asking each other if you've seen the 'metastatic chamber'. I have not seen the metastatic chamber. There's nothing I've come across that was immediately recognizable as a metastatic chamber, the way all other things present their names to me.

The drivel gives a message of coloured rings and names. You see yourself suspended in space, and a coloured ring appears. The ring flies off towards a star, as a name echoes in your mind. The ring colours seem to correlate to the three unbreakable tools I made in the jungle. They are all rings, and they are the colours from the vision. If I match the colours up to the unbreakable rings, according to the kwish's message, the coordinates I've been collecting are for the blue ring. But, what would I do with the blue ring?

The narn vision piques my interest the most. It seems to show a use for the quilbert. At least, I think it's the quilbert. I never would have thought it would be possible. I must test it.

There has to be another area in the city. I've walked out to the tarmac and looked over the buildings. One building is taller – it holds the second floor. The tower is tall, but you can't see anything in there. The walls are slick, no footholds or ladders or any way to see if there is more than the floor I sleep on.

I'm going to go through the tools again, then the buildings, room-by-room. If the metastatic chamber still exists, I'm going to find it.

USING MY NOODLE

There is more to the ground level than I knew and also another use for one of the tools. First the new use, because it is amazing.

I am in the Osmotic building because I have a theory about a connection to it and one of the tools. I brought my journal with me, in case I needed to take notes, like this note. While here, I decided to look at my reflection. I hadn't bothered with that since Endoon and I discovered the changes the tools make. Leaning over the Osmotic, I could see my appearance showed me flamboyantly dressed with an antenna. I don't have an antenna. The lower level tool I was holding made me look that way. Only higher level tools, it seems, show my true

reflection. I shuffled my tools until I was holding a noodle –
the high level tool, not the food – and my mind drifted to
Endoon. How he thought it was my species that constantly
changed appearance. As I thought of him, my mind was
overtaken, filled with a vision.

I could see through Endoon's eyes. I'm sure it was
him. He was moving through the jungle, low to the ground,
as a zleen would be, stopping and sniffing. I could smell the
rich jungle air. In his peripheral vision I saw a statue go by,
but to him it was nothing. It was like walking past a tree. It
was insignificant. Up ahead I saw another zleen. It was
waiting for him. When he reached it, they nuzzled each
other's tiny black noses and took off through the jungle. I
returned to my own body.

Was that my zleen with Endoon? If the noodle
can---

TRAPPED BY A CRAZY PERSON

In my last entry I said I discovered more of the ground floor. I am currently trapped in that area. There is a crazy woman on Beautiful Zurt. While I was writing the last entry, I felt a breeze go through the room. The last time that happened, Endoon showed up. Knowing that, I ran out to see if someone had teleported down.

From the glimpse I got of her, I would guess she's a bounty hunter. Maybe she's after Endoon, but she shot at me. At me! For what reason? None.

When I ran out to see if someone was here, I left the Osmotic building and headed through the Foonball Emporium. I saw her out in the courtyard. She was wearing armored gear and a helmet, a gun in her grip, resting the barrel on her shoulder. She saw me and fired a shot. It didn't hit, so I guess it was only a warning. I ran through reception, grabbing my escape bag, out of the gate to the jungle, then north around the city wall and in the north gate to the Osmotic building. I opened and closed the new door. She can't get in here. It would take her months, even with the best blaster she has.

You might wonder why I would go back into the city. I could have tried to lose her in the jungle, but with the loops, I might end up right in front of her before I had a chance to get away. Even if I could outrun her, I can't outrun a blaster. I'm hoping the exit makes her think I've run into the jungle. No sane person would come back in another way. I'm hoping she thinks I'm sane.

I have a dongle with me. It's a small purple sphere with holes in it. It helps project your voice but doesn't give away your location. There's an ad for it in one of the other tools. I pulled it out and gave a shout.

"I'm not your enemy. I'm stuck here too!"

Gunshots. Hope she has a lot of ammo with her, if that's her only means of communication.

"You can't leave. No one can, unless we work together."

Repeated, angry gunfire. I hope she's watching where she's firing. She better not be chipping up my walls.

I considered saying nonsense until she ran out of ammo, but some bounty hunters are known for making their own projectiles from whatever they find on any given planet.

"When you're ready to act like a civilized entity, let me know!" I can be brave, when I'm behind a foot thick wall and the person with the gun doesn't know my location.

That was the last thing I said. She replied with more gunfire. I haven't heard anything since. I must have dropped the noodle in the dash, because it isn't with my tools. If I had it, I could see her location. I'll have to make another one.

The area I'm in looks like a night club. Nine rooms total, three of them with dance floors. One room has a roulette wheel. It still spins, but it's not much fun betting against yourself. One room has a Grinfrazzitz. I was glad to see a machine in here. Thought I'd be here all by myself.

I pushed the button on the Grinfrazzitz as soon as I saw it. The doors to the room shut. If that bounty hunter does get through the main door, I could hole up in there, but I'd have to do it before she's through the main door. The Grinfrazzitz doors close slowly. She could easily make it through if I don't time it right. I pressed the button again to open them. Instead, the whole room started vibrating violently and everything I was holding flew out of my hands. That might come in handy. The third press opened the doors again.

I'll admit it. I did some dancing in the rooms to the south. The rooms are full of coloured sparks that shoot out of the walls and swirl around you to staccato music. I think they singed my hair. As you dance, the sparks change colours. Okay, so I didn't know that would happen when I started dancing, but I can use it as an excuse for why I kept dancing. Problem is, I still had the dongle on me. I'm not sure what I said exactly, but at one point I was dancing and singing things like, "There's a crazy bounty hunter on my planet." There wasn't any gunfire, so maybe she's moved to the basement or jungle.

I'm bedding down for the night on the tables in the middle room. They're big metallic purple slabs like in West, and just a hop to the Grinfrazzitz room – in case she figures out where I'm hiding. I have enough supplies to last for quite a while in here, if I have to. I'll give her some time to cool down and realize the situation.

Just woke with a start. The moolkoo message is about the Grinfrazzitz!

And the dance rooms - they are the cubes where the aliens dance in the Freenish vision! Blue for power. That was the impression that lasted from the vision. Blue for power. I don't want to forget that, so I'm writing it down.

SPARK CHAMBERS

The cubes are the spark chambers in the Freenish vision. I spent the morning dancing. The lights change colours as you dance. Each chamber remains the colour you stop on, as long as you stay in the chamber. I tried dancing all the colours to blue, then---

CRAZY, BUT SMART

The crazy woman is a quick study. I was making my notes on the spark chambers when she started talking to me. She was using a dongle!

"Where are you, alien?" I guess she meant me. I'm the only one she's seen on the planet, as far as I know. I waited a little while. I didn't want her to realize she could talk to me so easily. She called out again.

"What do you want?" I tried to sound a bit bothered, angry, as though I were busy.

"Let me off your planet, and I won't kill you."

"You've obviously found my notes. You know neither of us can leave here – unless we work together."

"Don't lie to me, alien!"

"Renya."

"What?"

"My name is Renya. I'm sure you saw it in the papers. You could try to be the tiniest bit polite."

That was met with silence. I've heard nothing since. I waited. I think she may have thought she could track me if she could get me talking. I guess she'll have to try something else. She can't be smart enough to build a dongle and use it, yet not realize I'm stuck here too. I don't know what she might be having a go at now.

~ ~ ~

Nothing from the crazy woman for hours. If she has my notes, she's probably using the tools to find any place she thinks I may be hiding. Since my only notes on these rooms are with me, she'll never find me. Unless she finds these rooms the same way I did.

THE BARON IS ALIVE!

The Baron is alive, though I'm not sure where he is. I don't recognize the place. There was really nothing to recognize, besides the Baron.

I built a noodle to see the location of the crazy woman. I thought of her and could see through her eyes. She's in West, going through the paperwork. She seems to be getting frustrated reading my notes. I was sure I wrote them in English but, through her eyes, some of them are in the alien language. I may have adapted too well to this planet. Perhaps, I am the alien now.

After the image of her faded, I thought of how I got here. Then, of course, I thought of the Baron. My vision was filled with a place of grey-blue mist. There was a glow around me. I could feel that I was alive, and something seemed to whisper to me of great power, but all I could see was the mist and the glow. I was floating, in a state of slowed heart rate and thin consciousness, but alive – soundly alive. It reminded me of the sensation you have as you come out of long haul sleep.

There is a mist room in the basement. This was not that room. That's the only misty place I've seen. It must be on Beautiful Zurt, because the tool is from here. It is some place *other*. Perhaps in the loops in the jungle. I didn't hear insects. I didn't hear anything, except some subtle whispering of powerfulness.

I'm going to build a scroom. I'm leaving the rooms and heading for Endoon's gun. If the woman tries to stop me, I'll hit her with the scroom. That will give me time to get out to the cylinder. When she first came down, I thought I could convince her to help, now I want her out of the way. I will find the Baron on my own and get us both off this planet. But first, I'll get rid of her.

Bounty Hunter 1 – Renya 0

There's a lump on the back of my head. My elimination of the bounty hunter was not a success. I'm in West. I woke up here about an hour ago. Endoon's gun was still in my hand. I don't know how I got here after she knocked me out. Nonce, my head hurts.

The bounty hunter is in the Hall of Whispers, meditating. As soon as I woke up, I crept around with the gun looking for her. I found her there in the center of the floor, sitting lotus style. I aimed the gun to fire but, in a swift fluid movement, she pulled her blaster and pointed it at me. To me, it didn't even look like she opened her eyes.

"Please. I'm learning," was all she said. I stood there, the gun on her, thinking I could still shoot her, but she might be able get off a shot before me. I lowered the gun and came back here.

There's a chunk of time missing – more than an hour or so.

I remember getting ready to leave the hidden rooms to hunt her. Before I left, I checked the noodle again. She was still at the desk in West with my papers. I slipped through the portal into the Osmotic room. By shuffling along the wall, I managed to get past the Osmotic without him bellowing. I dropped my bag and extra tools on the walkway outside his building and made my way to the north gate. I was careful, even in the jungle, because she could have left the reception room. Endoon's gun was still in the cylinder. I took it out and made sure it was loaded. I walked quickly along the wall of the city to West Reception and came through the gate with the gun out. She was not there.

I made my way through the buildings, slowly, with the gun leading. If she knew I was looking for her, she could be hiding in wait. I glanced around each doorway before entering. Through the Foonball Emporium, the map building, down the dog-legged hall. She was nowhere on the ground level.

The elevator with the mongoo flashes continuously. I remember deciding it was a better bet than the egg chamber. I made my way to it, and got off when the light was less – basement level. I stood in the low slung hallway, listening. I could hear the coils humming. She had put a torkus in the hopper. When I first did that, I went straight to the coils. The sound drew me there. I thought, with any luck, it had drawn her as well.

The light was off in the dark hall, but I'm familiar with the layout, and I knew to walk lightly on the stone floor to not give myself away. I stopped at the edge of the door, peering in the hopper room to be certain it was clear. Carefully, I went into the room. I was sure she would be right outside the door to my left – looking at the coils. I made my way to the faint portal, ready to fire.

That's the last thing I remember, before I woke up in West with Endoon's gun still in my hand.

Morriah, the Bounty Hunter

I was right. She is a bounty hunter, and she was looking for Endoon. I told her his fate, but she doesn't believe me. Can't really blame her. Who would believe he won an animal from a machine, put it in another machine, turned into that animal, and is now living in the jungle? It's a little out there. Seems like the ridiculousness of the story would make her realize it has to be true. I have no allegiance to Endoon. Why would I help him escape?

She's gone through the city looking for him, then ventured out into the jungle a bit. Didn't take her long to see that wasn't for amateurs. About four hours after she left, she was back, leaves in her hair, dirt on her boots, but no Endoon. I took the time to edit through my notes. I haven't told her about some tools. I didn't realize how much I haven't written down, until I looked over my papers.

I had to win a zleen to prove there was such a thing. I couldn't talk her into taking it down to the chute. Don't think I didn't try. I released the zleen into the jungle. It wouldn't be right to force it to live in the city. I hope it finds the others. I hope Morriah doesn't find any of them.

Morriah – that's her name. That, and her occupation, is about all she's told me. She stomps around here like a Galdayan trooper. She keeps her blaster on her hip, but I don't think she'd use it. I returned Endoon's gun to the cylinder. She'd left it in my hand, after she knocked me out, partially as a show of faith and partially because she said she couldn't pry it from my fingers. After her time in the Hall of Whispers, she's been going through the notes and papers again. If she asks me 'Did you try...' one more time...

She doesn't know about my journal. I don't want her reading it. The journal stays in the inside pocket of my jacket, tucked away with my travel documents.

At first, she thought I worked with Endoon. I told her a friend had sent me a message about this planet, and that's how I ended up here. She didn't believe it, straight off.

"Your friend... Endoon?" She asked.

"If Endoon were my friend and got me trapped on

this planet, do you seriously think I wouldn't give him up to you in a second?"

"You're saying a different friend invited you into this trap?" Ouch.

"A different friend who needed help."

"Where is this friend now? Did he turn into a creature and run off into the jungle as well?"

"No. He's around here somewhere." This made her suspicious. Maybe I had a whole crew hiding out somewhere to jump her. I wish I did.

"So there are other people here?"

"Not here, no."

"In the jungle?" She asked.

"Nope. He's here. I'm just not sure where."

"When your friend shows up, will I be able to see him?" Could be she thought I'd lost my mind while I was here. As long as I've been stranded here, it was a possibility. I came so close to showing her the noodle, letting her see through the Baron's eyes herself, but I might need to use that on her sometime. Plus, I don't want her to be able to track me anytime she wants.

"I have to find him, before I leave." I said.

"You think you might know how to get off this planet?"

"I have some ideas, but I won't leave without the

Baron."

"The Baron?"

"Yes."

That line of questioning stopped immediately. She knows the Baron. I could tell. I could tell as soon as I said it. As soon as she accepted 'Yes' as a response. There was no 'The Baron, who?'. I could tell by the way she looked at me out of the corner of her eye the rest of the night. The way she moved straight on to the tools and their uses. She knows Baron Hylke.

NEW EYES

I'm at my vacation home – the Blub. I've been working with Morriah for several weeks now. Devices needed recharging. I told her I'd be back in a few day. She's been out here, but I think we could both use some time away from each other. We can work fine for a few days, then the bickering starts.

"What does the nebbish do?" Morriah, shuffling sheets of paper.

"Nothing." I pick up a few tools and start breaking them apart and attaching them.

"It can't do nothing. Everything does something." Her tone gets tense.

"Somethings don't do anything." I keep at my task. When she starts getting frustrated or bossy, I don't let it get to me. Bounty hunters are like wild animals. To her, this planet is a cage.

"You must have missed something. What did you try?" She turns around to face me. I hand her the nebbish I made while she was griping.

"Here. Have at it."

That's when I walk away and let her realize sometimes I'm right.

Of course, I'm not always right. I have to give her the credit she deserves. She saw something I hadn't seen. I mapped the city and the jungle with the ceeveese. I noted every location number, but eight numbers are missing. I haven't used the map in so long, I never would have caught it.

We've gone over it again and again. We've walked the jungle to every loop, every artifact. We've looked for other hidden rooms. The locations aren't accessible. Seven of the numbers are in sequence. That implies another area, maybe another floor, or group of hidden rooms. One number is outside the sequence. The numbering starts on the second floor, picks up in the basement, except one number is missing. We've search the second floor and the basement with no sign of any areas I haven't found.

If there are eight coordinates missing, and the Baron is in some place I haven't found, that lone coordinate is my best guess on his location. The area where I saw him didn't seem to be a series of rooms. The big question is how to find the hidden places. We've been racking our brains. She's trained in hunting. I'm trained, mostly self-trained, in exploring. Between us, we should be able to figure this out. There has to be something we've missed.

~ ~ ~

Earlier today, while we were in the jungle, I decided to ask Morriah about the Baron.

"How do you know the Baron?" Direct enough. Plus, I made sure it was completely out of nowhere, to catch her off guard.

"Who?" She kept walking, but there was a split second stop. I saw it.

"Come on. The Baron knows a lot of people. You happen to be one of them. So, how'd you meet?" She came to a full stop but didn't turn to face me. There was a struggle going on. Even without seeing her face, I could feel it. It really wasn't any of my business, but not telling me would only make me want to know more. I couldn't tell which way it would go.

"I haven't seen him in ten years." She still didn't turn, but her head dropped. "Omnese. I was with him on Omnese."

I must have gasped, because she glanced over, then back down. Omnese was one of the planets the Baron had marked in my com as unsafe. One of the planets he set my com to alert, if I ever drew near it. One of the planets the Baron made sure I knew the name.

"We lost everyone."

"Everyone?"

"He never told you?" She brought her head up, still not turning towards me, but looking determinedly straight ahead.

"No."

"Maybe that's for the best." She started walking again.

I wanted to know more, but it didn't feel like the time to keep asking. Who was everyone? Who is Morriah? Why was she with the Baron? Ten years ago was five years before I met him.

I tried guessing her age – it was hard. As a bounty hunter, she's in top form. She could be his wife, his daughter, maybe another apprentice he'd taken on. Why haven't they talked since? Was whatever happened his fault, or hers? She hasn't seemed any more or less willing to help find him. She knew the missing coordinates might help, and she didn't hold back the information when she spotted it. What if she's been looking for him all these years to exact some type of vengeance, and I lead her right to him?

~ ~ ~

On my way back to the city, I'm going to take a

little detour. There was something I was going to try, seems like months ago, before Morriah landed. I'm not sure it will work, so I didn't bring the exact tool. Morriah might have noticed. I'll make it in the morning.

HUMANOID'S BEST FRIEND!

I have a gwirg! I mean, I am holding a gwirg in my hands. Well, not right this second. It's sitting beside me on the ground. I had to set it down to write, but I held it for quite a while before I was willing to set it down. I'm on a hillock in the jungle, a ways from the city.

As I said last night, there was something I wanted to try. One of the tools seemed to imply there was a way to capture a gwirg. It even described the tool. It worked! The gwirg, normally a calm robot with its chirping 'This way to the Oolgorboid' chant, turned and snarled, then jumped into my hands and ate the tool!

I think I'm still shaking a bit. After it ate the tool, I wasn't sure it would stop there, but I didn't want to drop it either. I stood, holding it out from my body, until I was sure it was safe. When I calmed down a bit, I held it up over my head in triumph and... it lifted me, only a tiny bit, then back down again. I tried it repeatedly, aiming it at the sky. Each time it would lift me some, then return me to the ground. Perhaps the circumstances in the jungle aren't right for it to work properly.

I have tried asking it to take me to the location number I believe holds the Baron. It didn't recognize the command. There must be a way to get there. The teleporters in the city only go to the basement and second floor. Maybe some other device, that seems to do nothing, will work. I'm going to have to try them all.

Also, I have a gwirg!

MORRIAH AND CORNELIUS

There is a third person on Beautiful Zurt. A fourth if you're still counting Endoon. I don't count him anymore. The new guy's name is Cornelius. He arrived while I was in the jungle. When I got back, I came in through the force field around the tarmac. You can come into the city that way, but you can't go out. I heard some noises in the Hall of Umflungoo. I couldn't imagine Morriah was playing one of the games. I showed them to her, but she didn't care. She has rations on her. I figure once those are gone, she'll care. She looks at the crackers like she thinks they're poison. She's seen me eat them for weeks. She should know they're safe.

I made my way to the hall and found a young man

playing the game. He was tall, lanky, with a flop of blond hair. He had no gun, not even a gun belt. He looked like a day explorer.

"I don't know these words!" He shouted, laughing.

"You will, eventually!" He seemed a little too happy for someone who just found out he's trapped on a strange planet.

"Can you help?"

I looked at the wall and recognized the word, shouting it out. A flungoon popped out of the machine. The walls lit up with my name. I picked up the flungoon and handed it to him.

"You're going to want the flungoon. There are delicious crackers inside." I told him. I held out my hand.

"I'm Renya."

"Cornelius." He shook my hand. "This place is amazing!"

"You do know the planet is a trap, don't you?" I asked.

"I could explore for months!" He walked around the room looking at everything closely.

"Have you met Morriah?"

"Yes. She said she was busy, and I should go to the Hall of Whispers to learn the language."

"And you did?"

"No. She just pointed. I tried to find it, but I got side tracked. The other game is super hard!"

"Yes, it is."

At this point, I was starting to question Cornelius' sanity. He was way too excited about being on Beautiful Zurt.

"Let's go see what Morriah is up to, then I'll show you the Hall of Whispers."

"Okay."

Morriah was walking around West with tools scattered all over the floor and desk. She looked up when we came in.

"That's a gwirg!" She ran up, touched the gwirg, ran her hands over its smooth, spherical surface. "How did you...?" She looked up, truly surprised. I had forgotten I was carrying it, what with the strange new person.

"I wasn't sure it would work, that's why I didn't mention it. I heard you met Cornelius?"

Morriah waved her hand as though to say 'Oh, him'.

"What does it do?" She asked me.

"I'm not sure yet, but when I aimed it at the sky, it tried to lift me."

"May I hold it?"

I handed it to her. She held it gingerly as though it might break.

"How long have you had it?"

"About a day now. I got it out in the jungle on the way back from the Blub."

"But, a gwirg came through here, not thirty minutes ago." As she spoke, she spun the gwirg in her hands, tweaked the antenna, admired it.

"Maybe something produces more, like the Oolgorboids?" I suggested.

She handed him back to me. We both looked up to find Cornelius gone. I turned to Morriah, and saw her touch her gun as she pushed past me for the exit.

We found Cornelius standing in the center of the Hall of Whispers. He was staring at the ceiling when we came in, then looked over at us.

"So, I listen to the voices?"

"Yes." I replied. Morriah glanced back at me. She seemed to sense there was something strange about this guy as well.

"Okay, see you guys in a while. Wait, how long does it take?"

"Took me about five hours. Does that sound right, Renya?" I nodded. I never told Morriah it had taken me weeks to learn the language because I didn't know sitting in the Hall of Whispers would do it.

Morriah and I looked at each other. I shrugged. We left Cornelius there.

Back at West, I walked carefully around the tools Morriah had spread out on the floor and set the gwirg on the only clear spot on the desk.

"When did Cornelius arrive?" I asked.

"Don't know. He walked in the room about an hour ago and said hello." She said.

"Did you feel a cool breeze, right before he got here?" I asked.

"A breeze? No, there wasn't a breeze. Does that mean something?"

"When you teleported down, and Endoon, I felt a breeze, one that shouldn't have been there. That's how I knew something was going on."

"I don't remember a breeze." She shook her head, thinking hard.

"Any idea why he's so happy to be stranded here?" I asked.

"He is, right? I thought maybe it was my impression, because I was busy, but he's exceptionally happy to be trapped." We both nodded, glancing towards the doorway.

"It's almost like he thinks it's a game." I said.

I asked Morriah if she'd found any new uses for the tools. She hadn't. She almost sounded apologetic. We tested the gwirg in West. Same effect as in the jungle – a slight lift, then return to the ground. Nothing substantial. I told her how I'd tried to teleport using the gwirg and it didn't work. We set to work trying to teleport with any of the non-known-use tools.

After about an hour, we were finished. None of them worked.

"That's everything, right?" Morriah asked.

"Yes." I sighed, then realized that wasn't everything. There were non-tools out in the cylinder. "The cylinder!"

She looked up, her eyes lit. We both scrambled for the door and out into the jungle. The three rings were a bust, but I am sure the blue ring is a major piece of the puzzle. Next was the rebozo. Morriah grabbed it first. She called out the teleport phrase we'd been trying. A vertical line of red fire formed a short distance from us in the jungle. It grew larger and larger, into a cylinder of fire, engulfing Morriah, and... she disappeared.

That was three hours ago. I haven't seen her since. If it took her to the coordinate she said, she's about three days out in the jungle. She was off one digit from the place that I believe holds the Baron. I don't know if she made a mistake when she said it, or if it was on purpose because she doesn't really want to find him.

I need to get another rebozo, but that would leave Cornelius wandering around here. I'm going to wait until he's finished learning the language and take him out to the jungle with me. I should be back before Morriah.

Gone Missing

I'm on my way back to the city to pick up the rebozo. I went with Cornelius to the orb. We made it out there fine. He didn't complain about the terrain, didn't need water, didn't seem to tire. I should have known something was wrong.

When we stopped to camp for the night I offered to make him a bed from the leaves. He said I shouldn't worry, he'd be fine. When I woke in the morning, he wasn't around. I was concerned, of course, that he may have gotten up before me and wandered off, but he came through the brush about a minute later. Everything seemed within the range of normal. He asked questions about the planet, how long I was here, how far I've gotten in the quest to get off the planet – things you'd expect, but something was missing.

"You seem pretty content being here." I said.

"I really like it. It's a great planet. I even like the name, Beautiful Zurt. It really is beautiful." He brushed his hand through the foliage as he passed.

"You're okay staying here for quite a while?"

"Yeah. I'm staying." Like he has a choice?

I thought he might have a mental disorder. Maybe he didn't fully understand the situation. I tried several avenues of questioning.

"It could be quite a while before we figure out how to get off the planet." I said.

"Yes, but I have faith that you will."

"Where does that faith come from?" I asked.

"Who knows where any faith comes from?"

If I didn't know better, I'd swear he'd been sipping Freenish juice.

Cornelius loved the orb. He dashed around like a kid when it started to swirl. He looked as though he was afraid he'd miss something. I had explained the mission to him, and Morriah's absence, but he seemed to think it was simply more fun things to do on Beautiful Zurt. He really saw the planet as a vacation destination.

It wasn't until we were halfway back to the city that things went sideways. We were making our way through the brush when he stopped. He didn't just stop, he froze. His face went blank.

"Cornelius?" No response. "Cornelius?" I grabbed his arm and tried to shake him – his arm evaporated in my hand. He was gone – just 'poof' gone. I looked around the area for anything. Did he trigger something hidden in the jungle floor? I couldn't find anything but dirt and leaves. I ran for a while after that. I ran until I couldn't run anymore. The city is still a while from here, but I'm too tired to keep running. Maybe Morriah can make some sense of it, if she's still here. Maybe I imagined both of them. Maybe I have lost my mind.

Back, Alone

I am back in the city. Morriah hasn't made it yet, if she's real. I made a noodle, to see where she is, but if Cornelius and she are both figments of my imagination, couldn't the noodle show me what I want to see? With the noodle I could see she was still a half day south of the city. She must have taken a few wrong turns.

I have the rebozo and am ready to test it, but I'd like to get her account of using it before giving it a try. I also need to make sure she's real.

I was thinking I might need another rebozo. If they only teleport the person holding it, I'll need another for the Baron – if I find him. But, if I leave now to get it, Morriah will come back to an empty city. Even if she guesses where

I've gone, she'll know I should have been back by the time she got here.

Pieces are either coming together, or everything is falling apart. I really don't know which.

IF I DON'T RETURN

Morriah returned from the jungle. She took a side trip to the orb to get another rebozo. I have two now. As far as I can tell, she is real. Cornelius is a whole other matter. Neither of us can explain what happened to him. She asked if I'm sure he didn't turn into a zleen and run off into the jungle, but she was kidding. I think she finally accepts that Endoon is gone.

I'm teleporting from the jungle. I don't know if the cylinder of fire is safe inside the buildings. Morriah is more than willing to let me be the one to check the coordinate. She said it was a slip of the tongue, when she said the wrong number.

"Could it be you don't want to see the Baron again?" I asked.

"I think it would be best if you are the first person he sees." She avoided my eyes, looking around the room, over her shoulder, as though someone might sneak up on her.

"Why?"

"We didn't leave on the best terms."

"Should I tell him you're here?" Her head shot up.

"No! Wait... I don't know... " More glancing around.

"Tell me what happened. You know. He knows. I'm the only one who doesn't know. If we all know, it's done." I wanted to get on with this.

Morriah moved over to the desk and sat down.

"The Baron... is my father-in-law. His son, my husband, was part of the crew we lost on Omnese." She squinted and looked away. "It was our honeymoon voyage. The Baron promised us a trip we'd never forget."

"I'm so sorry." I searched for words with more meaning and drew a blank.

"I don't blame him, not now, but I did, for years. I cursed him, screamed, yelled, all of it. It took a while for me to realize he'd lost a son, his only son. I didn't want to see that at the time. I was in too much pain myself to see his pain." She looked down, ran her hand over her eyes quickly. "He'd lost his wife years ago. I knew how cautious he was, but I still blamed him. There's no way he could have known.

"Jason, my husband, his son, he teleported down while we were sleeping. He never came back. A few of the crew went after him. When they didn't return, we knew there was trouble. Our last man went down – he had to sedate the Baron to keep him from going down himself – he sent a message 'They're all dead. All of them', then his com stopped sending. I pulled us out of orbit, and we were at the nearest spaceport before the Baron came around. I got off there. I left him with no one. It was selfish, but it was all I could do at the time."

"I'm sorry." I didn't know what else to say. The darkness I sometimes saw in the Baron's eyes made sense. Would he be glad to see her, or terribly sad for what she represents?

"You traveled with the Baron for a while, didn't you?" She looked at me, puzzled.

"Yes. A couple years. Why?"

"I didn't think he'd ever take on crew again. I'd heard, through mutual friends, he swore off traveling with anyone. He didn't want the risk."

"He warned me of planets to avoid, taught me everything he knows." I told her. "If it weren't for him, I don't think I would have made it exploring on my own."

"We should get on with this." Morriah said. She stood up, took a deep breath, and headed for the door.

We are right outside the gate of West, getting ready for me to teleport. Morriah's getting a little antsy at me taking the time to write. It calms me. I don't know what's going to be on the other end of this teleport. I don't know if I'll be back.

I am leaving the journal with Morriah, in case this doesn't work. I think she deserves to know everything I've learned. I guess she could be reading this in a minute. I hope I quoted you properly, Morriah. Maybe there's something I put down that will help.

I'm off to get the Baron.

We Both Thought Cornelius Was Real

Renya has not returned from whatever that coordinate holds. It's been a full day. At first, I waited. Then, I decided to get a rebozo and go after her, but realized I might be adding another body to a smaller trap. An hour ago, Cornelius came back.

That's right, Cornelius is back. But, Cornelius is not real. He's a hologram.

The real Cornelius is in high orbit above Beautiful Zurt. He has a fascination with planetary advertisements and heard Renya's distress signal. He is a very cautious traveler – sending down a hologram before teleporting onto an unknown planet. He zapped out that day in the jungle because his ship started dropping to a lower orbit. A lower orbit would have forced him to teleport down and he would be stuck for real, like Renya and I.

Cornelius doesn't know what pulled the ship in, but he plotted a higher orbit, and took some time to do scans of the planet. The scans show one building is higher than it appears from ground level. Knowing this, I took the gwirg there. Cornelius couldn't follow. Even knowing the exact location, he is unable to project his hologram into the building.

I aimed the gwirg and found the hidden coordinates – all except the one where Renya went. They are definitely the master control rooms. This is what I found:

Room 1: A gold chamber – one portal east, blue force field for three other walls

Room 2: Carpeted room – plush carpet, strange music, portals leading east and south

Room 3: An observation chamber – this is east of R2 and has a star field

Room 4: Machine room – cramped, full of machinery

Room 5: Chrome room – slick, chrome everything

Room 6: Entrance to Metastatic Chamber – 'Authorized Personnel Only'

Room 7: Metastatic Chamber – a panel with lights

and a button.

None of the lights were lit. The button is locked in place.

I got back down the way I went up. Cornelius was waiting outside. I'm not sure what to do. This journal is almost two years worth of notes. There is no way I can find anything relevant quickly. On some pages, I can't read Renya's writing. I think she wrote mostly before she passed out at night. A lot of it looks like scratch.

If Renya doesn't come back, I'll have no choice but to try reading this or start over. Cornelius thinks he can scan in the journal and convert it to readable text. He scanned a few pages, but many of the entries are in the alien language. His system is having trouble converting the handwritten alien text. Though Cornelius learned the language, his computer did not.

WHAT MORE DON'T I KNOW?

Renya is with the Baron – they appear well. She neglected to tell me about using a tool called the noodle. She is a clever liar. There were several times I asked about tools, only to be told 'Some things do nothing'. In this case, that was not true. I do not understand the area where she and the Baron are located. They seem to be floating in a mist. I sensed no immediate danger.

While I was using the noodle, I thought about Endoon. He is a zleen, living in the jungle. He is no more than a zleen anymore. I doubt anyone would give me the reward for turning in a small, furry creature.

Cornelius has tried sending his hologram to the location that holds the Baron and Renya, but that coordinate is inaccessible to him as a hologram.

There appears to be four steps to escape. Cornelius is scanning the journal for any clues to those four steps. The tools are in levels – one through seven. There are non-tool items. There are two hoppers. Since the hoppers must play a part, there are two missing parts. I don't know if Renya discovered these parts. We have not gotten far enough in the journal to find that information.

RESCUE ATTEMPT TWO

I am going for the Baron, again. I am in the city now with Morriah. We are in the basement waiting for rebozos. Cornelius volunteered to go out for them. He is a hologram. He can appear at the orb with no effort. Though Morriah said there are areas that restrict him, most areas are open.

Morriah found the hidden coordinates while I was with the Baron. I looked over what she wrote – how many lights? – what colour lights? There are details missing. She said she will look again while I get the Baron. She seems nervous for his arrival. I don't know how that will go.

The location of the Baron is not mappable. When I made it there the rebozo I used to teleport was gone. It was

an odd sensation, floating in a mist. There were sounds –
voices maybe – and an overwhelming feeling of power. I
couldn't find the Baron at first. He was there, but all I could
see was a large cocoon, glowing blue. I floated around the
area, looking for anything else. The cocoon was the only
thing there. I knew it must hold the Baron. A personal
stasis device of some kind. I shouted his name at the
cocoon, to no effect. I touched it, and it sparked and stung
my fingertips.

I had only one remaining rebozo. Since the rebozo
requires a command from the user to work, I couldn't take
him with me even if I had another. I had to find a way to
waken him from stasis. I debated going back for more
rebozos, but noticed the glow of the stasis field was
dimming. It was slight, but it was dimming. Perhaps
touching it had an effect on it. It took several hours for the
field to dim enough to see the Baron through it. As it faded
completely, the Baron opened his eyes, at last.

"Renya! You've found me!"

"You're alive!" I had feared he wouldn't come out of
stasis well.

"How long have I been here?" He asked.

"I don't know. I don't even know where *here* is."

"How long have you been on Beautiful Zurt?" He
looked around, like someone who wakes in an unfamiliar
house.

"Almost two years." I reluctantly told him.

"Two years? Have you solved the puzzle then?" I understood the worry in his eyes.

"Almost. We should get out of here. I brought two rebozos, but one is gone now." I tried to hand him the rebozo. "You take it and teleport to the city." As soon as I made the offer, I realized it probably wasn't the best plan. Morriah was waiting. He had no idea.

"No, no. You go back and bring three. I've been here long enough to be comfortable a few more hours."

"Are you sure?" I was sure, but I couldn't stop myself from saying those words.

I have to tell him about Morriah, but decided I will wait until we are ready to go to the city together.

AND THEN IT EXPLODED

We are safely in the city. It was a difficult conversation, telling the Baron Morriah is here. I waited until we were ready to teleport.

"The location is 288, but there's something you should know..." I flipped my rebozo over in my hands, shifting from one foot to the other. I couldn't look him in the eye.

"Renya? What is it?"

"There's someone else here. Someone you know." I looked up. His eyes tightened. Maybe he knew who it was, or was thinking of someone else he didn't want to see. He didn't ask who. He stared at me like I'd broken a prize possession, and he was waiting for me to confess.

"It's Morriah."

He let out a low whistle. I'd heard him do that before in tight situations. Once, while we were traveling together, we landed on a planet where they tried to hijack our ship. We were given the choice of turning over the vessel or tracking down a prisoner and killing him. They didn't have the equipment to do it themselves. If we didn't do it, they would commandeer our ship to do it themselves. Our fate was vague for that choice. The Baron let out the whistle, then agreed. We would do it. Only, we didn't do it. He spent hours with them going over the plan, me getting more and more nervous about it, and in the end, we teleported to our ship and left at top speed. If he hadn't persisted in detailing the plan, they may not have believed him. He is a good actor, at times.

"How did this happen? Did you call for her?"

"No. I didn't even know who she was." That didn't seem enough. "I would never do that," I added. "She's a bounty hunter now. She was chasing someone who ended up on Beautiful Zurt."

"You're joking? Morriah is a bounty hunter?" He laughed. This was a good sign, right? "I guess she learned a thing or two from Jason." His laughter died out. The glint in his eyes dimmed. Memories taking over. Memories of his son, and how he lost him.

"I know it's been a while." I said. "I know this will

be hard. She doesn't blame you, not anymore. And, she's been helpful. There are things I couldn't have done without her. This is a lot to take in right now, but you can do this. If you can't, you can fake it. I know you can do that."

The glaze left his eyes. He reached out across the mist and pulled me into a hug.

"That's my girl, Renya. You know the Baron." He let me go, patting my arm. "Thank you. Thank you for believing in me enough to get yourself mixed up in this and not leaving me here."

"It really was a rotten thing to do." I said.

"It was a terrible, rotten thing to do. However, there was no one else I trusted enough to come and get me. No one else." He smiled. "Let's go see what other messes I can make."

The reunion was much what I expected, at least from the Baron. An awkward hug in greeting. Then, 'we should talk'. I suggested the second floor, because it's the quietest area in the city.

I could have waited to see the end result of the conversation, but I was curious. There's a tool I hadn't used before. It's called a fashnork. It's pretty remarkable. It makes you invisible. I never really had a use for it. Or, I should say, I never had it handy when I could have used it. Yes, totally wrong to listen in on their talk, but what was the harm? All I had to do was take the teleport to the second floor and push the button on the fashnork. I wanted to see how the conversation was going.

I found them in the chapel, sitting side by side. I stood by the doorway to listen.

"He was always impetuous." The Baron said.

"I wonder where he got that from?" This made the Baron chuckle.

"I tried to teach him caution over impulse," the Baron said, "but example can be stronger than words."

There was a quiet pause.

"I'm sorry, Morriah. I should have locked the teleport."

"He wasn't a child. He made the choice to go down there." Morriah was almost whispering. "I don't blame you, Baron. I don't think I ever really did. I needed to be angry at someone..."

Then, the fashnork got blazing hot in my hand and exploded with a flash of red light, leaving me standing in the doorway in a cloud of burnt insulation smell with a shocked look on my face.

They both turned to look, then the Baron burst out laughing, long and hard. Morriah started laughing along with him.

"See how well I teach them?" He asked, still laughing.

FOUR LIGHT PANEL

I've been to the last hidden rooms. They are beautiful. Morriah didn't do them justice. The first room is a pulsing gold platform with a force field on three sides. It leads into a room with plush carpeting and ethereal music. I imagine this was the waiting area to teleport out. There's an observation chamber with a view of a star field. It's stunning.

Three of the areas are mechanical. One room is so full of machinery you can barely move. I don't think anyone is supposed to be in there. From the size of the aliens in their videos, they either used robots or some other creatures to service the machinery. Maybe that's why the Osmotic gives zleens? The last room is the metastatic chamber – solid chrome ceiling, walls, floor. It takes your breath away. I hope it will take all of us away.

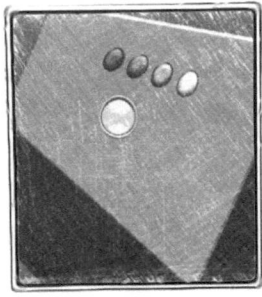 The control panel is up there. The console I saw in the vision. There's one button. It glows a faint blue. It's locked in place right now. Four lights, four colours, and I know what we need to do to light up all of them. At least, I think I do. A lot is resting on me.

We all feel like we'll be leaving soon, but if I've gotten anything wrong, we could still be here for a while. My main concern is the spark chambers and the dome. There are three of us who want to leave – Cornelius can leave at any time – it will take five people to activate everything, at the least. To feed the hoppers and work everything else would take seven. That must have been the minimal staffing, when Beautiful Zurt was up and running.

The Baron came up with an alternative.

"Cornelius, what do you do if something goes awry with your hologram?" He asked.

"Why, I make another. It's simply a matter of pulling the 3D file from backup."

"And, if you wanted to make an extra?"

Cornelius took a second. Morriah and I turned towards him. We understood the plan.

"Multiple holograms... I think it's possible." Cornelius said, then blinked out.

"I like a man who gets straight to work." The Baron said.

~ ~ ~

We tried a test run. The Baron manned the main console. We use the dongle to communicate over the distances. We filled the hoppers first. They're active for a while after they're switched on. I filled the hopper in the basement. The light lit on the main panel. Morriah had to see the drivel vision about three times before she trusted me on filling the golden hopper. She got the buttons to light, flipped the switch and the whole board started beeping wildly. The second light lit on the main panel. I worked the dome. Light three came on. Morriah and I ran from one spark chamber to the next. It wasn't enough to light that button. We got three of the buttons lit. The metastatic chamber made sharp crackling sounds, but with no occupant and no spark, it fizzled out.

If Cornelius can figure out how to project multiple holograms, we have a chance. Three people leaving means we have to do this three times, and each time with one less person. We'll need four extra holograms and Cornelius, for all of us to make it off.

We were hoping to enlist Cornelius as the rebozo maker, but he hasn't returned yet. The more rebozos we have, the easier it will be to get everything else we need. Just in case, I'm out at the orb right now. I touch the orb, wait for it to finish spinning, then use the dongle to see if Morriah has gathered the rebozo. We'll need a lot. For the golden hopper it would take over a week to gather the objects we need, if we had to make the trips on foot. If Cornelius doesn't come back soon, we'll gather everything and set it out on the ready.

The Baron has been going over my notes. He said later tonight he'd like to have a look at the Freenish. He hadn't found that, and he's fascinated by the thought of it.

~ ~ ~

There has not been anything, in all my time here on Beautiful Zurt, as delightful as seeing Baron Tarris Hylke sipping Freenish juice, except watching him stumble through the jungle under the influence of a vision. I guess it may be because we can see escape in view. We're all feeling a bit lighter in mood.

"This is quite wonderful!" He said after sipping the juice. "And in a while it will take effect?"

"Yes." I replied.

"Well, let's make our way back then!" He walked a short bit, then started swaying.

"Baron?" Morriah asked.

"Oh, my!" He said. I laughed. I couldn't stop myself.

Each vision seemed to catch him off-guard, though he knew full-well the effects of the Freenish juice. If he didn't persist in trying to walk under the influence, it might not have been so funny. Morriah and I laughed until our sides hurt.

Central Intergalactic Switching Network

Cornelius came back today. He only has enough equipment to produce three holograms, including his own. Since three of the duplicates need to do the exact same thing, I've asked him to try splitting one signal into three weaker signals. He thinks he can do it.

He has found a major problem with our escape. While working on the holographic projection equipment, he had his system run a search for any historical documents pertaining to Beautiful Zurt. The planet has gone through several names, been terraformed, and was finally abandoned over 100 years ago. There are rumors and vague references floating around that the original occupants moved to another planet after selling Beautiful Zurt to a developer hoping to make it a resort. A news story here and there mentions the opening day. A few years later, all news dried up.

Through all the years it was in use, Beautiful Zurt had gone through several contracts with switching networks to teleport visitors out. There's something in the atmosphere that makes normal teleportation off the planet difficult without the use of an outside service. The last switching service they used sent out-going teleports to GalaxEnter. That's why all the information, coordinates and devices on the planet point to that service. However, GalaxEnter went out of business about the same time as the last mention of Beautiful Zurt in any articles. With no switching station, Cornelius isn't sure where the teleport will take us – it may scatter us across the outer atmosphere.

Cornelius has gone back to his ship to work on splitting the hologram. If he can accomplish that, he's going to try pulling the Baron's ship out of low orbit. The Baron has a lot of sophisticated equipment he might be able to use. He wants to see if he can find a way to hone his teleporter onto the outgoing signal from the planet and scoop us out of thin air.

The mood here is sullen. We have nothing we can do to help. We have to stay and wait for word, and we all know what the risk will be for the first to try teleporting out.

Of course, the Baron stepped up to be the first to try

it, but I won't let him. He and Morriah are family. They've found each other after all these years. There's no way I will let either of them be the first to go. It should be me. I have no family. I've never had a family. The Baron is the closest I've ever come. But Morriah is his real family, and that matters more.

THE WAITING TIME

Morriah and the Baron have been catching up on lost time. He's even talked her into playing Umflungoo and Foon-ball. The Baron is surprisingly good at Foon-ball. I've been wandering around the city. I guess I'm saying goodbye.

I didn't realize I was wandering, until I found myself in the basement at the traset box. I opened it and took out a traset. I rolled it around in my hand. The metal tubes clanking against each other with that jingle-jangle tone. We have all the items we need to try the metastatic chamber. They are all sitting at the ready, right next to where they go.

Cornelius has checked in a few times. He has the

Baron's ship in high orbit and can teleport between the Baron's ship and his own. With all Cornelius has been doing to help, it was still hard for the Baron to give up his passcode to allow a teleport reply from his ship. He finally whispered it to him. Cornelius is going to wait until we're off the planet to try to retrieve my ship and Morriah's. He's worried about mine because it's a very small vessel. His attractor might crush it. Getting us off of Beautiful Zurt is more important than our ships. I understand that. Morriah, not so much.

I'm leaving for the jungle in a few minutes. One of the articles on GalaxEnter's teleportation system says we can take only one thing with us – required – and nothing else from the planet. I can't take my gwirg. I really wanted to take my gwirg. Rather than teleport out to the jungle and get them, I volunteered to make the hike. It will take Cornelius a few more days of work until he's confident his teleporter can snatch our signals. He's been teleporting things into space around his ship and pulling them back with the altered system. So far, they've returned imploded, twisted, and misshapen. We do not want to come back that way.

Besides it being a goodbye tour of the jungle, the time and space will give Morriah and the Baron a little more time to catch up.

THE LAST OFF THE PLANET

I am bedding down for the night in the jungle. My jungle. My jungle on my planet. The planet I will soon leave.

No one knows this planet the way I do. Of us, the Baron was the first to arrive, but he gave up early. He was here a few months, then surrendered. Rather than solve the puzzle that is Beautiful Zurt, he put himself in stasis and waited for someone to rescue him. How could he do that? I suppose the loneliness got to him.

Morriah has been here several months. She's worked hard to help find a solution, but all of the work we've done since her arrival was built on the work I'd done. Yes, there are things I couldn't have done without her, but her time here is still short compared to mine. She doesn't stop to touch a statue on the way to something else. She doesn't take a traset from the box every time she's in the basement. She doesn't stare at the coils, taken in by the sheer beauty of them. She doesn't go to the chapel to watch movies, just because. She doesn't see any of the charm of Beautiful Zurt. She doesn't even look up when a gwirg comes in the room.

I shouldn't fault them. They haven't lived here – not really *lived* here. They've been stuck here, stranded here, striving to get off – but not living. They haven't spent years collecting water from the cistern for daily use. They never ran their fingers over the scratches near the teleport slot wondering about everyone who came before and put their coin in to go to the second floor. I suppose I've only had the experience I have, because there were many, many times I was sure I would not be able to leave. I made myself at home. And now, I will leave this home.

Endoon will remain here. Endoon will inherit Beautiful Zurt. Inherit it from me. I will relinquish my planet to him. The only life form that will live here when we are gone will be the zleens in the jungle. If they are life forms.

I have what I came into the jungle to get. I'll head back to the city in the morning. We will leave, maybe not tomorrow, but very soon. I will be the first to leave. I told them I would, but really I'd prefer to be the last. Whoever leaves last will likely be the final person ever to set foot on Beautiful Zurt. We are going to deploy warning beacons around the planet. Though people ignore planetary broadcasts, warning beacons are always heeded.

I don't know how I can get out of being the first to teleport off. I insisted so much. Maybe if I act a little afraid, Morriah will step up. She likes to prove her strength of character. I used to try to prove mine, but it's a draining endeavor with no real reward except danger. It seems wrong to go against my word, but I want to be the last. It's my planet. They should give me that.

READY TO LEAVE

Cornelius is ready to grab us from thin air. If there were two of me, I would go first and last. I will dweezle the Beautiful Zurt tools we've made before we go. No sense leaving them laying about. I'm photographing all the tools before I dispense with them. We've gathered up all our paperwork. The Baron asked me to scan and transcribe his notes and give him a digital copy. I think he senses my hesitation to leave.

"You'll write this up, maybe submit it to Planetary Review?" The Baron asked, as we gathered the papers in bundles.

"I don't know about submitting it, others might want to come here."

"You can make sure they understand the risk." He said. "Unless... you don't want them here?"

"Oh, I don't mind." I looked up. The way I said it, the way he asked it, we both assumed it is my planet. "It's not like I own the place."

"No. I don't think anyone really owns it." He stopped, looked around the building as though scanning the whole planet. "But you may be its last living resident."

I laughed. That's what I am, not the owner, but the curator.

"You should talk to Cornelius. He could show you his hologram system. You could come back any time you want."

"It wouldn't be the same." I told him.

"But, it might be a good way to reminisce."

The Baron has never teased me for my sentimentality. I think he realizes, since I grew up in the system with no family, I form attachments to strange things. Sometimes the oddest thing can be very special to me, like the gwirg. I will really miss the gwirg.

The system isn't a home, it's a bed and meals and basic education. All the archaeological digs were the same as the system – bed, meals and work with an education. My first home was with the Baron. He taught me a lot, but that wasn't the only reason I traveled with him. He looked after me and helped me. It wasn't the same as the way the system teaches you to avoid danger. He really cared that I didn't come to harm. My second home was my own ship. I do miss my ship. I hope Cornelius doesn't crush it. My third home is here, Beautiful Zurt. And I'll be missing that soon enough.

Tomorrow morning we'll all teleport out. I couldn't bring myself to argue or pretend I am afraid to go first, so it's still me, first off the planet. If I make it, Morriah will follow and the Baron will be last. We were going to have Morriah and the Baron work the hoppers while I teleport, but sometime while I was in the jungle it was decided that Cornelius would take care of all of it. All we have to do is show up in the metastatic chamber. Cornelius can't get in there, so we'll all wait for the lights to light, then I'll take my place in the transfer chamber, they'll press the button, and we'll see if I end up on Cornelius' ship or scattered in space.

ARRIVAL

We were waiting in the teleport area, each of us holding only what we needed to leave. Morriah reminded me to take the cacapoo out of my hair. Nothing extra from the planet to transport out safely. The lights began to light on the console. We stared at them. One, two, three – all four lit, and I was about to step towards the transport chamber when the Baron pulled a scroom. Morriah's blaster came up, out of instinct, but she lowered it quickly.

"What are you doing?" She snapped.

"I should be the test." The Baron said. "All of this was my doing. I want to make up for some of it."

"Don't be ridiculous." I said. "We're all leaving.

Cornelius is sure we'll be fine."

"Then, there's no argument." The Baron motioned with the scroom for us to move away from the transport chamber. We edged along the wall to the control panel. "Just to be sure." He fired the scroom at us and our Oolgorboids went flying, then he stepped into the chamber. He looked back, tossed the scroom on the floor, and winked. "One of you press that big blue button there, will you?"

Morriah reached across the panel and pounded the button. The chamber lit up bright white. The Baron seemed to break into tiny sparkling spots of light, and then... he was gone. We waited – seconds passed as minutes.

"I have the Baron!" We heard Cornelius shout through a dongle to us. We neglected to bring one, so there was no way to ask details about the transfer. The lights on the panel started to illuminate again.

"Do you mind?" Morriah picked up an Oolgorboid.

"No. I'll shut off the lights, figuratively." I said.

She smiled and stepped into the chamber. The four lights glowed. I pressed the button. That's when I realized there was a slight flaw in the plan. Who would press the button for me?

The metastatic chamber lights dimmed down. Morriah was gone.

I looked around the room. Snatched up my Oolgorboid.

"Got her." Cornelius called.

Three gwirgs and a scroom. I glanced at the panel, three lights were lit. I had to toss a gwirg. The scroom wouldn't do it. They don't weigh enough. I scooped up the three gwirgs and set them right outside the transfer chamber. It's a big button, but I had never tossed a gwirg before.

The panel was lit – all four colours. It was time to go. I stepped into the transfer chamber and picked up a gwirg. I tossed it at the panel. It bounced off. I wasn't even close. I grabbed another, tossed it. I saw it strike right next to the button, then shift a bit. Did it?

I didn't have time to question it. I was suddenly sliding through something like a space water park. Twists and turns, a bump here and there, a spiral, a drop and then a dead stop. A voice boomed in my head.

"You have reached the Central Intergalactic Switching Network. What are your coordinates?"

I shouted the coordinates. My own voice sounding muffled in my ears. My brain was reeling 'Was that right? Did I get them right?'.

There was a bright flash of light and my body, my molecules, felt as though they were being tweezed apart, like no teleporter I'd ever used. My consciousness floated for a second, watching my body disassemble then reassemble. It floated down into the newly formed body, as my surroundings came into focus. Three figures, not quite clear, but recognizable as living beings.

"That'll give you a headache, huh?" Morriah said.

As my vision sharpened, there was one person I didn't recognize. Tall, pale blue skin with black short hair almost like feathers.

"Cornelius?" I asked.

"Oh," he said. "Yes. I forgot to warn you. I hologram according to the lifeforms I find on a planet. Gave the Baron quite a start."

"I've seen worse." The Baron said.

"But it was a bit unexpected." Cornelius said.

"I wasn't sure where I'd ended up!" The Baron said.

Cornelius laughed, leaned over his controls.

"I'll pull in my holograms, then we'll see about those ships you ladies left circling about."

It will be good to see my ship again.

EPILOGUE

Cornelius pulled my ship out of orbit with only a dented thruster. Morriah wasn't so lucky. It was almost as if her ship tried to fight the attractor. Once it was out of orbit, the Baron put it in tow behind his ship.

We had a dinner to celebrate. A big blowout with all our favourite foods, and a few things from Morriah's chiller that wouldn't fit in the Baron's.

The Baron set out the warning beacons. We argued over the colour. Orange means very dangerous, red means deadly. The Baron thought it should be red. Beautiful Zurt isn't deadly. It's a lot of things – annoying, inconvenient, difficult – but not deadly. An orange beacon is rarely set with a 'no return' signal, that was his reasoning. Rarely isn't never. I talked him into orange.

After a few days of rest and recuperation, we all gathered on the Baron's ship to say goodbye.

"We're heading to Statis9 Station. They should be able to repair Morriah's ship." The Baron said.

"Again," Cornelius said to Morriah, "sorry."

"It wasn't you." She told him. "That ship has always had an ornery side."

"What about you, Renya?" The Baron asked.

"I don't know. I think I'll head to a supply station, get some things I was thinking about while I was on Beautiful Zurt." I hadn't said the name since we got back. It made me sad. I had to keep talking. "I wish I could have brought a cracker back. I'd really like to get that recipe."

Cornelius laughed.

"I'm not kidding! You couldn't taste them." I told him.

"I'm headed to the GJ region. I heard of a small planet with singing plants." Cornelius said.

"Really?" I asked. He shrugged.

"You're welcome to tag along."

And you know what? I did, and the plants really do sing. If we ever cross paths, I'll play you the recording.

Gwingus
speckled ball with a button
wobbles for foonball

Mongoo
rod, always feels cold
for umflungoo

Snuge
cube with a button
says something?

Torkus
long, clear rectangle

Wigglesnort
small hexagon disc
brings the elevator

AFTERWORD

Would you like to walk the through the city where Renya Zaffor and her companions found themselves trapped? Do you think you could make it through the jungle? Would you like to make the tools, drink from the freenish, and see a real live gwirg tempting you to follow it to the Oolgorboid?

You can.

These fictional journals are based on one of the first multi-user adventure games ever created. Its proper name is Fazuul. It was written by Tim Stryker.

Fazuul is a text-based, science fiction adventure. It was first released in 1984, but is still available for play on a few internet based BBSs. Visit the Beautiful Zurt website for more information and plan your adventure.

http://www.beautifulzurt.com/

www.ingramcontent.com/pod-product-compliance
Lightning Source LLC
Chambersburg PA
CBHW031956170626
46807CB00006B/2507